## "You're going to marry her and take us to your ranch?"

**The twins looked up at Tate expectantly.**

"Not exactly." He spoke guardedly. "Look, your mom and I want to talk this over in private."

When they were alone, Blythe tried to hide her disappointment "I assume you're going back to Wyoming," she said, "and we have to decide how to work you out of my sons' lives."

"No. We have to discuss how to legitimize them," he corrected. "The long-lost, deeply abiding love of your past wants to see you," he said coldly. "I've come to take you back to him."

The color drained from Blythe's face, and she wondered suddenly just how far he would go to prevent her marriage to George.

With great effort she hardened herself against Tate, determined that he would not destroy her world....

H·A·R·L·E·Q·U·I·N

# FIRST·CLASS
*Sweepstakes*

## OFFICIAL RULES

1. NO PURCHASE NECESSARY. To enter, complete the official entry/order form. Be sure to indicate whether or not you wish to take advantage of our subscription offer.

2. Entry blanks have been preselected for the prizes offered. Your response will be checked to see if you are a winner. In the event that these preselected responses are not claimed, a random drawing will be held from all entries received to award not less than $150,000 in prizes. This is in addition to any free, surprise or mystery gifts which might be offered. Versions of this sweepstakes with different prizes will appear in Preview Service Mailings by Harlequin Books and their affiliates. Winners selected will receive the prize offered in their sweepstakes brochure.

3. This promotion is being conducted under the supervision of Marden-Kane, an independent judging organization. By entering the sweepstakes, each entrant accepts and agrees to be bound by these rules and the decisions of the judges, which shall be final and binding. Odds of winning in the random drawing are dependent upon the total number of entries received. Taxes, if any, are the sole responsibility of the prize winners. Prizes are nontransferable. All entries must be received by August 31, 1986.

4. The following prizes will be awarded:

   (1) Grand Prize: Rolls-Royce™ *or* $100,000 Cash!
   (Rolls-Royce being offered by permission of Rolls-Royce Motors Inc.)

   (1) Second Prize: A trip for two to Paris for 7 days/6 nights. Trip includes air transportation on the Concorde, hotel accommodations...PLUS...$5,000 spending money!

   (1) Third Prize: A luxurious Mink Coat!

5. This offer is open to residents of the U.S. and Canada, 18 years or older, except employees of Harlequin Books, its affiliates, subsidiaries, Marden-Kane and all other agencies and persons connected with conducting this sweepstakes. All Federal, State and local laws apply. Void in the province of Quebec and wherever prohibited or restricted by law. Winners will be notified by mail and may be required to execute an affidavit of eligibility and release, which must be returned within 14 days after notification. Canadian winners will be required to answer a skill-testing question. Winners consent to the use of their name, photograph and/or likeness for advertising and publicity purposes in conjunction with this and similar promotions without additional compensation. One prize per family or household.

6. For a list of our most current prize winners, send a stamped, self-addressed envelope to: WINNERS LIST, c/o Marden-Kane, P.O. Box 10404, Long Island City, New York 11101

# The Wyomian

## Betsy Page

# Harlequin Books

TORONTO • NEW YORK • LONDON
AMSTERDAM • PARIS • SYDNEY • HAMBURG
STOCKHOLM • ATHENS • TOKYO • MILAN

Original hardcover edition published in 1984
by Mills & Boon Limited

ISBN 0-373-02730-3

Harlequin Romance first edition November 1985

# CHAPTER ONE

DURING his years as a private investigator, Harvey Adams had dealt with all types of people, but there was a quality about the rough, dark-haired rancher who sat watching him through coldly penetrating grey eyes that unnerved the seasoned veteran. Maybe it was the angry hardness of the man's weather-worn features which gave him an air of maturity and authority far beyond his thirty-four years, or maybe it was the uncompromising line of his lean square jaw or the cutting edge of his gaze. Whatever the reason, for the first time in Harvey's career, he was hesitant about delivering his information. Sitting in the wood-panelled study with its racks of guns sandwiched between the bookshelves, he experienced a deep sensation of guilt as if he was lining up three helpless prey for the slaughter.

Reaching over the walnut desk that separated the two men, Tate Calihan accepted the blue folder Harvey had been clutching dubiously and began leafing through the pages of the carefully prepared report. 'I'll read through this more closely later. Why don't you give me the highlights.' It was a command, not a suggestion.

'I picked up her trail in the small town you mentioned in northern Missouri. She had returned to stay with her aunt and sister until the boys were born.'

'Boys?' Tate interrupted with a frown.

'She had twin boys,' Harvey elaborated, feeling slightly superior by coming up with information that obviously shocked his client. 'Identical twins. Like two peas in a pod. But she's not twee about it. She doesn't dress them exactly the same, and all that. Even if she did, it wouldn't

5

take long to tell them apart. The one named Roger is a real rounder with his shirt-tail aways out and his hair messed up. Brian is quieter, but I did notice he was quick to enter into any of Roger's mischief. In fact, I sometimes had the impression that Brian was the brains behind some of their more elaborate schemes.'

'You've actually seen them yourself?'

For a brief second the detective was certain he caught an unguarded note of curiosity in the cowboy's voice. 'Sure. You asked me to handle this case personally and, as you are a friend of Neil Solane's, I was happy to oblige. Mr Solane sends me a lot of business.'

'Could we get on with your report, Mr Adams.' Tate's cool exterior had returned and there was a briskness about his manner that indicated that he found the entire situation distasteful.

'Of course, Mr Calihan,' Harvey frowned. 'Soon after the boys were born, the aunt and sister died in a car crash. The aunt left her the house and some insurance money. She sold the place and bought a condominium on the outskirts of St Louis, and has been living there ever since with the boys. She works in a local branch of a large bank that's within walking distance, and the boys attend second grade in the local public elementary school.'

'What name does she use?'

'Her own. Blythe Walters.'

'What about relatives?'

'None she is close with. Her parents died when she was ten and she and her sister went to live with the maiden aunt I mentioned a minute ago. With the death of that aunt and her sister, she was left essentially on her own. There might be some distant cousins scattered around the country, but I didn't think you were interested in them. You did emphasise current information.'

'I'm not. What about friends?'

'She keeps in contact with the doctor from that town in northern Missouri, but other than that she seems to have severed her ties there. There's a middle-aged widow named Ethel McFay who lives in the condominium downstairs. She's pretty thick with them. Takes care of the boys after school until their mother gets home from work. I gather she has baby-sat for them since they were infants. The boys have the usual array of school friends and Miss Walters has a couple of females from work she eats lunch with occasionally, but generally they keep pretty much to themselves. Nice little family group.'

'Male friends?' The question was curt, cutting off any further editorial remarks the detective might have been considering.

Harvey moved uncomfortably under the man's steady gaze. 'She sees a man by the name of George Lansky. He's working as the assistant bank manager at her branch right now, but it's only a learning position. His family owns the whole operation.'

'Does he stay over much?' The insinuation was blunt.

'Never. She's not that kind of woman. She's a good mother and, like I said, they're a nice little family group—one any man would be proud of.' The detective's tone was defensive. He felt like the white knight defending a defenceless maiden and her brood.

'And you are certain she's the woman I hired you to find?' A cynical smile curled the lean man's mouth.

'The name's the same and she's the image of the girl in the photograph you gave me.' Anger flashed in Harvey's eyes. He resented having his competence questioned.

'Thank you, Mr Adams.' Tate Calihan rose and extended his hand, marking the end of the interview.

'There is one item on your bill I think I should mention,' Harvey said as he accepted the handshake. 'Standing around on the street, or even sitting in a parked car in that neighbourhood, draws a lot of attention, and you were clear about not wanting the lady to know she was being observed.' He emphasised the word 'lady' and paused for the cowboy to confirm this instruction. The man nodded impatiently for him to proceed. 'The way the complex in which they live is set up is that each building houses four condominiums—two upstairs and two downstairs. The two upstairs share an adjoining hall and staircase. As I mentioned before, the lady lives on the second floor. The old couple who own the neighbouring condominium rent their place for the winter while they go down to Florida. They wouldn't agree to a short-term lease, so I had to take the place for the entire winter season. Also, the McFay woman supports herself by running a cooking and cleaning service, so I hired her. This gave me the opportunity to question her without her realising what was going on. She likes to talk while she works. Anyway,' here he reached into his pocket and pulled out a key, 'the place is yours now, unless you want me to continue my observation.'

'No, I think I have all the information I need. I appreciate the job you've done.' There was finality in the words.

'If you ever need my services again, feel free to call,' Harvey delivered his usual parting line, only this time he hoped the man would not call again. This investigation had left a bad taste in his mouth. At the door he hesitated, wanting to say something more in the woman's defence, but the look in the Wyomian's eyes told him that this was not any of his business. Besides, he didn't know what he was defending her against, so without any further delay, he turned and left.

Tate Calihan sat staring at the photograph affixed to the blue folder with a paper clip. 'So she had twins and she kept them,' he muttered aloud. 'How very convenient.'

Four weeks after Tate Calihan's final interview with Harvey Adams, Blythe Walters was cleaning up the Forbes' place. As she finished wiping down the shower stall in the bathroom off the master bedroom, she gave thanks to all the people who had developed inoculations against most of the childhood diseases, then added a silent prayer that someone would come up with one for chicken pox, even though it would be too late to help her.

Straightening up from her crouching position, she ran her thumb under the waistband of her jeans to remove an uncomfortable wrinkle, and pushed a loose strand of hair back under the red-and-blue bandana tied around her head. Turning to step out of the shower stall, she froze, a gasp of fear catching in her throat as she came face to face with a tall stranger leaning nonchalantly against the door-frame, studying her with a pair of grey eyes which lost their look of masculine approval and became suddenly shuttered.

'Sorry to startle you, ma'am,' he drawled as he removed the tan stetson from his head in a gesture of politeness, his eyes remaining on her hand which clutched the bottle of cleaning fluid.

'Who are you and how did you get in?' she demanded, forcing her voice to remain steady as she braced herself in the small enclosure and tried to remember if she had locked the front door. She hadn't. She had left it unlocked in case Ethel needed to send one of the boys over for her.

'You made my entry very easy by leaving the door unlatched. However, I do have a key.' Raising his hand slowly, the man displayed the small silver object. Although he made no sudden moves and appeared to be maintaining a relaxed stance against the doorjamb, Blythe did not miss noticing the tan fabric of his trousers tighten against his legs as the muscles of his thighs tensed.

'Having a key doesn't tell me who you are.' Her eyes

locked on his face, she began to unscrew the lid of the bottle in her hand. The man stood a good six inches taller than she, and the calluses on his hands told her he wasn't one of the soft urban cowboys who dressed like cow-punchers, but had never punched anything more solid than his pillow.

'Name's Tate Calihan and I'd be much obliged if you'd put down that bottle. You're making me a mite nervous.'

He said the name as though he expected her to recognise it. She didn't. And although she ceased in her action of removing the lid, she did not put the bottle down as he requested. 'How did you get the key to Mr Adams' place?'

'Harvey Adams was doing some work for me. However, it has reached a point where it is necessary for me to take over.' Then, indicating the bottle with his eyes, he asked, 'Do you mind if I straighten up? This doorjamb is starting to feel hard on my shoulder.'

Nodding her approval, Blythe was beginning to feel foolish. Still, there was something about the man she did not trust. 'Why didn't Mr Adams tell Ethel you would be coming instead of him when he called last week to ask her to make certain this place was clean and the kitchen stocked?'

'Guess he forgot to mention it.' As Tate straightened, his muscular frame blocked the doorway for a moment before he moved away, out into the bedroom and then down the hall. Blythe followed slowly, glad to be free of the confines of the bathroom. Two suitcases sat on the living-room floor. Removing his suit jacket and loosening the string tie he wore, Tate unbuttoned the top two buttons of his shirt. 'I've told you who I am. Would you mind introducing yourself?'

'Sorry. I'm Blythe Walters,' she threw over her shoulder as she walked through to the kitchen to put the cleaning materials away. 'I live across the hall.'

'Have you taken over Mrs McFay's cleaning service?' He had followed her and was now filling the kitchen doorway.

'No. I'm merely doing her a favour. I have a job at the local bank which I much prefer.'

'I see.' He moved only slightly to allow her to pass, forcing her shoulder to brush against his chest. The flesh beneath the white cotton fabric felt granite hard and, glancing up into his face, Blythe had the impression that there was nothing soft about this man. 'I was also informed that meals would be provided when requested. Are you doing the cooking for Mrs McFay, too or is the cleaning taking up all of your spare time?'

'Ethel did mention that Mr Adams was having her prepare his dinners,' she responded hesitantly. 'And, since she was able to find other people to cover her other homes, I guess I could take care of providing your meals. I do feel responsible, and she is my friend.'

'Responsible?'

'The reason Ethel can't do her work right now is because my boys gave her the chicken pox.'

'And how does your husband feel about your cleaning up after strange men?'

'I'm widowed.' Her reply sounded natural. She had made it so many times now, it was beginning to feel like the truth.

'You are very young to be a widow. Was his death recent?'

'No. It happened several years ago.' There was something in the man's tone, as if his show of sympathetic concern was forced, that caused her response to come out sharply. Changing the direction of the conversation she asked, 'Do you want din—'

The question was interrupted by a loud pounding on the door followed by the wooden structure being thrust open and a small brownish-red head peering in around it. 'Mom, you've got to come fast! Brian's stuck in the closet and he's getting real upset.'

'How can he be stuck in the closet?' she demanded of her second son as they crossed the hall into her living-room. The inquiry was rewarded with a shrug of a small shoulder.

'I'm sorry, Blythe.' Ethel was standing in front of the closet door in question looking close to tears, her face and arms still covered with drying pox sores. 'They were watching cartoons so nicely. I dozed off.'

'It's all right,' Blythe assured her. 'Why don't you go on home and get some rest? I'll take care of this.'

'Who are you?'

The question exploded from Roger in a tone of intense interest as he looked past his mother to the man who had followed them.

'I'm Tate Calihan.' The cowboy knelt down to the boy's level and extended his hand in greeting.

'I'm Roger. Roger Walters,' the child beamed, and as the small hand was encased in the larger one, Blythe was puzzled by the sudden flash of emotion in the hard man's eyes. However, she quickly brushed the feeling off by telling herself that he simply liked kids. And right now she suspected that Roger was going to need all the friends he could find because Brian could not have got himself locked in on his own.

'Mom. Help! It's dark in here!' came a plaintive cry from the closet.

'Don't be frightened,' she soothed through the door. 'I'll have you out in a minute.' Taking a firm grip on the door knob, she pulled, but the door refused to budge.

'I've already tried that,' Ethel informed her. 'The door is stuck solid.'

'Mom!' The word was filled with tears.

'Brian, please, sit down and make yourself comfortable. I'll have you out in a few minutes,' Blythe directed while wondering how she was going to keep that promise short of phoning the fire department.

'You have to take it off the hinges,' Roger offered authoritatively.

'I have to what?' she questioned, looking sharply at the boy.

'You have to take it off its hinges,' he repeated, a slight nervous tremor in his voice.

'And how would you know that?'

'Because that's what the custodian at the school had to do.'

'The custodian at school?'

'Yes, ma'am.' Roger looked away, avoiding his mother's gaze.

'Mom!' The voice from the closet sounded close to hysterics.

'Just hold on, Brian,' she called back. 'The door has to be taken off of its hinges. It's going to take a few minutes.'

'Do you have a hammer, a screwdriver and a pair of pliers?' Tate asked.

'I'll get them,' Roger offered, leaving the group to return only moments later with a metal box containing an assortment of equipment.

Blythe moved back to give the man room to work, and catching Roger by the arm dragged him with her in spite of the protest in the boy's eyes. Working deftly, Tate had the door loose within minutes. With seeming ease he grasped the structure and carefully removed it, leaning it against the adjacent wall.

Brian shot out of his temporary prison and into his mother's arms where he remained only momentarily before turning towards his brother and giving him a look which promised revenge at a near date.

'I'll put the door back on now,' Tate remarked in a slow easy drawl as he reset the wooden structure on its hinges and reinserted the long screws. 'I have a feeling it won't stick again.' Blythe caught the warning look he threw at Roger and was surprised by the boy's chastened obedient nod. She also noticed when Tate slipped an object from the floor into his pocket.

'It had better not,' Brian hissed towards his brother.

Ethel, who had ignored Blythe's suggestion that she leave, nudged her friend on the shoulder. 'Where did you find him? He's certainly a cut above George. If I were twenty years younger I might even consider giving you some competition.'

'He found me.' Blythe's cheeks flushed slightly as she recalled the encounter. 'It appears that Mr Adams was working for him and he has decided to take over the project. He'll be staying in the Forbes' place now.'

'How very nice for you,' Ethel commented with an encouraging smile only to be rewarded with a cautionary frown from Blythe as Tate closed the tool-box and glanced towards the two women.

'That should fix it,' he informed them. Then brushing off his hands, he knelt in front of Brian. 'I don't believe we've met. I'm Tate Calihan.'

'I'm Brian Walters and thank you, sir, for getting me out of there.' As the child shook the large man's hand, he added, 'I don't normally cry, but the smell of Roger's tennis shoes bothered my stomach.'

'I understand.' Tate nodded in a knowing manner bringing a smile to Brian's face.

'And I'm Ethel McFay,' Ethel introduced herself as the cowboy straightened to his full height.

'I guessed that,' he replied, with a smile that brought a blush of pleasure to the woman's cheeks. 'Mrs Walters explained the situation to me.'

'I hope you won't mind about Blythe taking over for me for a while. She's a very good cook.' Ethel's manner, which was more that of a mother promoting an available daughter than a business woman explaining altered arrangements, caused Blythe to shift uncomfortably.

'I'm sure she will work out just fine,' he returned indifferently, either ignoring or not having caught the inflections in Ethel's voice. Blythe couldn't be sure. There was a guardedness about the man. 'Now if you ladies will excuse me, I've had a long trip.'

As he strode out the door, Blythe followed, pulling her door closed behind her. 'Mr Calihan.'

'Yes, ma'am?' He turned to face her.

'First, I want to thank you for your help and, secondly, I'll take that crushed pencil you picked up off the floor.'

'He's quite a handful,' the cowboy noted as he dropped the splintered yellow wood into her outstretched palm.

'They both are,' she replied, adding in a warning tone, 'And they are both my handfuls.'

He nodded to indicate he had understood her meaning. Then, as she turned back towards her door, he said, 'I'd like to have dinner around seven.'

'Fine,' she threw over her shoulder without turning to look at him. There was something very disturbing about the man and she hoped Ethel would recover soon.

'Handy man to have around,' Ethel remarked, watching her friend closely. 'Quite a bit different from George I would say. It would be hard to wrap Mr Calihan around your finger. But then it might be a lot of fun trying.'

'I honestly don't think I'm up to the challenge,' Blythe responded drily, her tone putting an end to any further comments the woman might have been considering.

'I think I'll get that rest you suggested.' Ethel grabbed her coat and moved towards the door as she followed the line of Blythe's eyes to the backs of the two boys sitting in front of the television set, feigning engrossment in a sports programme. She hated family confrontations.

Switching off the set, Blythe stood in front of her sons, staring down on them angrily. 'You two promised me you would behave.'

'I'm sorry,' Roger spoke up quickly.

'It wasn't all his fault,' Brian admitted. 'I dared him. I didn't think it would work.'

'No television for the next seven days,' their mother stipulated. 'You realise that I might have been forced to call the fire department if Mr Calihan hadn't been here.'

'Is Tate going to stay until Mr and Mrs Forbes come back from Florida?' Roger interjected before she could continue her reprimand.

'I have no idea and it's Mr Calihan not Tate.' Her tone was firm.

'He won't mind if we call him Tate,' Brian offered matter-of-factly. 'He likes us.'

'He is Mr Calihan to the two of you and you are not to pester him.' Suddenly she felt the need to go outside for a while. 'Get your coats. We're going to the park.'

The boys looked at their mother dubiously, but did as she requested. This winter had been particularly cold and since before Christmas the temperature had not been above the freezing mark. Outside they were met by the frigid January wind, and their breaths showed white as they walked. A layer of Christmas snow still covered the ground, its top crusty, while patches of ice were everywhere. By the time they had reached the park and the boys had swung on the swings for only a couple of minutes, they were all ready to return to the warmth of their home.

Later, as she tried to concentrate on a murder mystery she had borrowed from one of the girls at work, the excursion out into the winter weather played on Blythe's mind and she realised that it had come about because she had felt the need to escape. What bothered her was that she had no idea what she wanted to escape from.

She and the boys were used to eating between five-thirty and six, so near five o'clock she started frying chicken for dinner. While placing four pieces of uncooked chicken in the refrigerator to be prepared later, she frowned. Cooking two dinners for the next week was going to be very inconvenient. Momentarily she considered asking Mr Calihan if he would consider changing his eating schedule, but shied away from that deciding that she could handle the situation for a few days. There was a quality about the man that made her hesitant about approaching him.

As Blythe turned the chicken and started the vegetables, a knock sounded on the front door. Knowing the boys would answer it and let her know if it was important, she didn't pay much attention.

'I don't mean to impose,' Tate Calihan's western drawl sounded from her kitchen door, startling her and causing her to spin around. 'But I woke up sooner than I thought I would, and hungrier.'

'You can eat with us, Mr Calihan,' Roger offered, standing resolutely next to the big man, attempting to imitate his stance.

'Call me Tate,' the cowboy requested, smiling down at the boy. 'I don't want to inconvenience your mother, but I would like to eat before seven.'

'Actually, it would be more convenient for me if you ate with us,' she confessed, then wished she had said she would bring his dinner over to him.

'In that case, I'd be pleased to stay.' The smile on his face as he watched her moving around the kitchen did not reach his eyes.

That was one of the things that bothered her about him, she suddenly realised. When he talked to the boys and to

Ethel there had been an openness in his expression, but from the moment she had turned around to find him watching her in the bathroom at the Forbes' place, there had been a guardedness about him when he looked at her. He made her feel as if she had an extra eye in the middle of her forehead or some other defect he didn't want to draw attention to, but could not overlook. This was an unusual situation for the pretty auburn-haired woman, and she found it difficult to deal with.

Tate had changed out of his suit and was now dressed in a heavy flannel shirt and old faded blue jeans pulled over the tops of his boots. Any minute, she expected him to take out a pouch of tobacco and roll his own cigarette.

'You're a real cowboy, aren't you?' Roger stared up at the man beside him, a look of deep admiration in his eyes. Brian had joined the others in the doorway and Blythe was struck by how natural the male trio looked together.

'I guess you could say that. I own a ranch out in Wyoming.'

'What are you doing in St Louis?' Brian questioned as if Tate had to be crazy to leave so splendid a place as his ranch to come to the city.

'I had some business to attend to.' There was a note in his voice which caused Blythe to look up from starting the second skillet of chicken. He was watching her with the same expectant expression she had seen when he had told her his name. It unnerved her and she felt the need to be rid of his presence.

'Why don't you boys take Mr Cal—Tate—out to the living-room and entertain him while I finish in here and set the table.'

'That's a great idea, Mom.' Roger grinned and, taking the man's hand, pulled him around and into the living-room. 'You can tell us all about your ranch. Do you know any Indians?'

Through the open doorway, Blythe saw the boys lead Tate to the couch and, climbing up on either side of him, give him their undivided attention while he told them about his home. Frowning, she wished that they would react to George in that manner instead of treating him like an outsider. Outsider. The thought stuck. George had been dating her for nearly a year now and he still felt like a stranger in her home. She had told herself that the boys would react to anyone coming into their tight little circle in that manner, but Tate Calihan was proving that theory wrong. The man had only entered their lives a few hours earlier and already the boys made it seem like he was a part of their world. 'You're still tired from the holidays,' she muttered aloud, 'and over-reacting.'

But when they sat down to dinner and Roger asked Tate to say grace in his place, and the man did, a cold chill passed over Blythe and she was thankful that she had a date with George the next evening to get her back on an even keel.

'Tate has a real Indian woman who cooks and cleans for him,' Roger informed his mother between bites. 'Her name's Ruth Fleetdeer. I told him about how I was an Indian in the Thanksgiving Day play at school, and he said he was sure Ruth would like to meet me.'

Blythe forced a smile.

'He's been telling us all about Wyoming,' Brian cut in, not wanting to be left out of the conversation. 'He says there's a lake there the Shoshone Indians call "The Lake That Roars".'

'But on the map it's called "Bull Lake",' Roger interjected, only to receive a frown from his brother as a reward.

'Anyway,' Brian continued, 'the Indians say that a bunch of white men were trying to kill a male white buffalo for his pelt but that the buffalo ran into the lake and drowned himself rather than die at their hands. So now during the winter you can hear his spirit bellow from beneath the water on windy days. Of course, that's only a legend. Actually, it's the wind blowing up under the ice that makes the sound, but I would like to see it sometime.'

'Maybe, sometime,' Blythe replied. 'But right now I would like for you to eat your dinner.'

The boys gave each other the look that said they knew she meant 'never', and with exaggerated sighs turned their attention to their food.

'I understand you have an exceptionally fine zoo here in St Louis,' Tate said, breaking the stilted silence. Immediately, the boys were once again beaming as both tried to tell him about their favourite animals.

'It's too cold to see much of the outdoor exhibits,' Brian noted with regret. 'The Bengal Tiger is really neat. His cage isn't really a cage it's a hab . . . habi . . .'

'Habitat,' Blythe aided her son.

'Right, a habitat, with rocks and grass and you can go up on a bridge-like thing and look down on him or, even better, you can ride the train around and when it stops at the station across from his lair he paces up and down like he wants to jump on all the passengers. Of course he can't because of the concrete river-like thing without any water that separates him from the fence.'

'The polar bears will be out,' Roger noted knowledgeably when Brian was forced to pause for air.

'We do go over for the inside exhibits once in a while,' Brian addressed Tate hopefully. 'Would you like to come with us next time?'

'If it's all right with your mother,' he agreed, much to Blythe's consternation.

'Terrific. How about tomorrow?' Roger suggested.

Blythe felt trapped. She was already feeling guilty about working most of the day today and, when she had been home, she hadn't been very good company. Then tomorrow night she had a date and wouldn't even be eating dinner with them. How could she turn them down? 'All right. We can go tomorrow, but Tate might be busy. He does have business here in town.'

'Can you come?' both boys demanded of the man in unison.

If he had caught the hint in her voice that she did not relish his company, he ignored it as he agreed to accompany them.

Later, as she washed up the dishes while the boys again entertained their new-found friend in the living-room, Blythe philosophically convinced herself that the trip to the zoo might work out well after all. She could have Tate come over for a big meal at noon, right after she and the boys came back from church, and then they could go to the zoo. Afterwards, she could feed all of them soup and sandwiches while she dressed for her date. That way the boys would have had a full day by the time Ethel came up to baby-sit and she would have fed Tate two meals which was one more than she would have normally prepared for him according to the arrangement Ethel had with Mr Adams. Of course, Mr Adams was not Tate Calihan.

As if he could read her mind, the man in question wandered into the kitchen at that moment. 'Dinner was very good.'

Blythe would normally have thanked a person who made such a comment, but there was an edge to his voice that hinted that he was surprised at her culinary abilities and it rankled her.

'I thought I would check with you about tomorrow,' he continued when she did not respond.

'If you mean the zoo, it's all right with me. I was planning to do something special with the boys anyway.'

'Actually, it's more selfish. I was thinking about my breakfast.'

'Breakfast?' The word came out in a startled, unbelieving tone.

'I was under the impression that Mrs McFay promised to make her full services available to Mr Adams.' There was a challenge in his voice.

'We go to church in the morning. If you want breakfast it will have to be before eight o'clock.' She met his challenge.

'I'm an early riser.'

'Fine! Dinner will be immediately following church at twelve-thirty and then after the trip to the zoo I planned to serve soup and sandwiches.'

'Sounds agreeable to me.' He received this less than polite announcement of the next day's eating arrangements with the barest hint of amusement, and Blythe had the distinct impression that he was enjoying making her life difficult.

Doing some fast figuring, she said, 'On weekdays I can fix your breakfast between six-thirty and seven and dinner any time after five. Lunches, you'll have to manage for yourself. I'll see that you have luncheon meats.'

'Six-thirty will be fine for breakfast and since my schedule is more flexible than yours, I'll eat dinner when you prepare it for your family.'

'Does that mean you'll be eating with us every night,' Roger demanded happily as he joined Tate in the doorway.

'That would be terrific,' Brian chimed in.

'I suppose it would be the most convenient arrangement for your mother. Then she wouldn't have two dining-rooms to clean up.' The innocence in Tate's voice did not ring true.

'Certainly. Whatever pleases you,' she returned, knowing she was trapped and not knowing how to get out of it short of out-and-out rudeness. Besides, he was right, it was the most convenient solution, and it was only until Ethel felt like her old self again. Surely that wouldn't be much longer than the promised week.

Tate left soon after this exchange and Blythe sent the boys to bed since they had to be up early for church the next morning. She, too, went to bed feeling more fatigued than normal. The whole day had been off balance, tilted. When she closed her eyes Tate Calihan's image came into sharp focus and she knew without a doubt that his presence had been the deciding factor in the disturbing texture of the day. He had shown up out of the blue, frightened her nearly to death, then made her feel ridiculous. After which, he had managed to become the centre of her sons' lives by performing a simple rescue. 'You're jealous. That's what your problem is,' she chided herself. 'The boys have never taken to anyone like they took to Tate, and you're jealous.'

She attempted to laugh at her foolishness but couldn't. Instead, she wished that George had been the one who had removed the closet door. Her life would be a great deal more comfortable if he was the one the boys were showering with hero-worship. 'No doubt Mr Calihan will soon tire of having two shadows at his heels and then life will calm down.' With that thought in mind, she said a silent prayer that Ethel would recover soon and drifted off to sleep.

The next morning dawned bright and cold. Blythe considered oversleeping by a smidgen, then remembered the extra breakfast she had to prepare and dragged herself out of bed. After brushing her slightly longer than shoulder-length auburn hair, and determining that nothing special would have to be done with it to make it look presentable, she pulled on a robe over her flannel pyjamas and trudged into the kitchen where she plugged in the coffee pot. Sunday was pancake day. With a yawn, she decided to cook Tate's breakfast in her own kitchen at the same time as she prepared the twins' meal, and then carry it over. If he wasn't ready for breakfast, or didn't like pancakes, that was his problem.

As she went in to wake up the boys, a loud knocking sounded on her door. Answering the summons, she discovered Tate standing there neatly dressed in a suit and tie, looking like he had been up for hours, and holding an empty mug in his hand. 'I do like to have coffee when I get up in the morning.'

'Well, I should think a man your age could plug in a percolator,' she returned snappishly, finding his presence decidedly masculine and feeling frumpy in her robe and pyjamas.

'That part I can manage.' He frowned. 'It's finding the coffee to put in the percolator at six o'clock on a Sunday morning that I find difficult.'

'Rats!' She clutched her head with her hand. 'When I stocked the kitchen, I put off buying coffee until I could find out whether to get caffeinated or decaffeinated and then I forgot all about it.' Seeing no other way to make amends, she opened the door fully and invited him inside.

Roger wandered out of his bedroom half asleep. 'What's for breakfast, Mom?'

'Pancakes, if I can get the batter mixed,' she answered, walking swiftly towards the kitchen.

'Tate!' The boy's eyes popped open as he became aware of the man following his mother. 'You coming to church with us?' he questioned, becoming the tail end of the parade.

'Depends. What church are you going to?'

'We're Presbyterians,' Brian announced proudly, having heard Tate's voice and immediately jumped out of bed to join the others.

'That's just the kind of church I was planning to look for,' the man confirmed, and both boys beamed.

'Just one coincidence after another,' Blythe muttered as she took his coffee cup from him and filled it. 'Milk or sugar or both?'

'Black will be fine.' He accepted the hot mug from her with a smile that did not reach his eyes. 'I take it that mornings aren't your best time.'

'Sometimes she's a little grumpy, but if you leave her alone, she mellows in a short period of time.' Brian noted in an authoritative tone.

'Thank you, my son, for coming to my defence.' Blythe threw him a half smile.

'She's mellowing already,' Roger announced triumphantly.

After starting the first batch of pancakes, Blythe set a third place at the table. 'You might as well eat with the boys since you're already here,' she informed the lanky cowboy who still stood leaning against the kitchen doorjamb drinking his coffee.

'Guess you're right,' he agreed. 'Besides, who could turn down so gracious an invitation.'

Frowning at herself, she made no retort. He was right. She was being antagonistic this morning and she wasn't sure why. Drinking a cup of coffee while cooking the pancakes, she blocked out the conversation between the man and the boys and tried to sort out her feelings, but gave up when the answers came out jumbled. The only thing that was clear to her was that she felt threatened by him. In a philosophical vein, she decided to blame this on their original encounter, telling herself that first impressions are difficult to shake. After serving each of the males a large stack of pancakes, and making sure the boys had milk and Tate had coffee and all three had orange juice, she poured herself a glass of juice and excused herself to go and get dressed. 'Yell, if you want more,' she instructed over her shoulders as she exited. 'There's more batter.'

Back in the privacy of her room she brushed her teeth, made up her face, and dressed, between sips of orange juice. Out of Tate's immediate presence, she was able to relax somewhat, although she did find herself glancing several times towards George's picture as if seeking protective support. By the time she had buttoned the centre button on the grey tweed jacket of the winter suit she had chosen to wear and pulled on the knee high black leather boots to protect her lower legs against the wind on the walk to church, she felt more like her normal self.

'Tate made us seconds,' Roger informed her as she entered the kitchen. 'He's a real good cook.'

She started to question the man as to why he wanted someone to wait on him hand and foot when he was perfectly capable of taking care of himself but, deciding that she had been shrewish enough for the morning, held her tongue. Tying on her apron before beginning to straighten the kitchen, she said, 'You two had better hurry and get dressed.'

'Those are fine boys you have there,' Tate commented as he sat watching her after the twins' departure.

'I think so.'

'I bet their father was real proud of them.'

'He died before they were born.' There was a bitter edge to her voice.

Undaunted, he persisted. 'Other than their hair which matches yours, I assume they look a lot like their father, or did he have auburn hair, too?'

Her grip on the glass in her hand tightened, whitening

her knuckles. Ignoring his question, she attempted to turn the conversation away from herself. 'What about you? Do you have any sons at home who look like you?'

'No. None that I'm aware of, anyway.'

His mocking smile caused a frigid chill to sweep over her. For men, bastard children seemed to be a joke. 'And I suppose you wouldn't care what happened to them if you did have a few scattered around without your legal name.' She glared at him.

'I would care very much.' His response was delivered with equal intensity and she turned away, feeling embarrassed and wishing she hadn't lost control.

'We're ready, Mom, Tate.' The twins announced in unison at that moment, saving her from the humiliation of trying to talk herself out of the accusation she had just made.

As they pulled on their coats, she schooled her voice into a more polite mode. 'There is an early service during the Sunday School Hour which I assume you intend to attend,' she addressed Tate. 'The boys and I will be going to Sunday School and the later service, so we will meet you back here around twelve for dinner.'

'I hate walking home from church alone. So I'll attend Sunday School with you and then go to the second service, too,' he corrected.

The boys were ecstatic while Blythe struggled to maintain her polite exterior. She suspected that some of the more ardent gossips in the congregation kept track of her activities, and up until now she had given them absolutely nothing to discuss. Tate, however, had a presence that could not be denied. There was no way they were going to miss him. Then there were the people from the bank who attended. Because of George's position, she and he had agreed to keep their relationship private. Therefore, it was not impossible to believe that one of her fellow employees might say something in front of him without realising he would be the least bit interested. Suddenly she frowned at herself. Gossips would find something to talk about with or without Tate, and George was going to have to find out about him sooner or later. The boys certainly weren't going to make a secret of their new friend. Stoically, she accepted the situation and, forcing a smile, followed the others outside.

Although the sidewalk was wide enough for the two children to walk abreast with one adult, the boys had apparently decided that Roger would walk to church with Tate while Brian walked next to their mother, and vice versa on the way home. Obviously, they did not want her to feel left out, and she smiled at their sensitivity for ones so young.

The boys introduced Tate as their new neighbour to everyone they encountered, saving Blythe from too many explanations. The Sunday School class was more difficult. Sara Taylor, one of several single women in the congregation, was the teacher, and she had an impossible time trying to keep her mind on the lesson and off Tate. While the others in the class found it amusing, Blythe found it disgusting, and was relieved when the class was finally over.

During the service the boys sat on either side of the man and, to Blythe's amazement, she did not once have to throw them a cautionary glance. They neither played with the hymnals during the sermon, nor made faces at each other during the singing. Following the service, several women, all either single or divorced, who usually didn't have the time of day for Blythe, stopped by to chat and meet Tate. He was courteous, but with both boys hanging on to him, none of the ladies had a chance to flirt and all left slightly disappointed. Blythe was tempted to mention that he was a man alone and could use a good home-cooked meal over the next week or so, but for some reason the words never came out.

The trip home was accomplished in a hurried silence. Although the sun shone brilliantly and the sky was clear, the wind was bitterly cold. Before leaving for church, Blythe had thrown a roast and vegetables in the crock pot to slow cook and, as they entered the living-room, the aroma was mouth-watering.

'I had the distinct impression that you were considering pawning me off on one or two of those women at church,' Tate said as he hung up their coats.

'I was,' she admitted before departing for the kitchen followed by a pair of curiously hard grey eyes.

'She was only joking,' Roger pulled on Tate's arm for attention. 'She doesn't even like them.'

'One of them, the lady with the short red hair, said we were probably bastards,' Brian frowned. 'I overheard her in the hall outside of our Sunday School room.'

'We asked Ethel what it meant because we didn't think we had been bad and besides, the woman wasn't even our teacher,' Roger elaborated.

'But she just got real red in the face and told us not to ask such questions,' Brian picked up the dialogue.

'After the way Ethel acted we decided not to ask Mom. We figured it would only upset her,' Roger finished as both boys looked at Tate expectantly.

But an explanation from that quarter was not forthcoming. Tate merely muttered under his breath, 'Some people are bastards through an accident of birth, and then there are those who are self-made.'

The boys looked at one another questioningly but, noting the hard set of the cowboy's jaw, probed no further.

# CHAPTER TWO

WITH Blythe as chauffeuse and the boys, sitting on either side of Tate in the back seat, acting as tour guides, they entered the grounds of Forest Park where the St Louis Zoo was housed. Snow covered the rolling hills, their deciduous trees starkly bare, while ice crusted the ponds and streams.

'There's a Planetarium here, too,' Brian said looking up at Tate hopefully. 'Maybe we could bring you to see that on another day.'

'Or the Jefferson Memorial,' Roger suggested. 'They have all kinds of guns and old fire engines and lots of stuff about Charles Lindbergh.'

'I admit, I would enjoy seeing those sights,' the man smiled back while Blythe frowned.

'If you stayed until summer we could go fishing, or rent a boat,' Brian continued enthusiastically.

'Yeah. There's all kinds of things we could do,' Roger chimed in. Then as Blythe guided the car into a parking space across from the brick wall of the zoo, he pointed towards the top of the hill to their right. 'The Art Museum is up there, and they have a real live mummy.'

'Mummies aren't alive,' Brian corrected.

'A real dead mummy, then,' Roger threw back.

Blythe shot them a warning look, hoping to prevent a confrontation. It was an unnecessary gesture, however, since they were both on their best behaviour for Tate. As they passed through the gate into the zoo grounds, the boys quickly pointed out the main train station where the miniature trains used to carry zoo visitors around to the various points were housed. The Polar bears were next, and although they were enjoying the weather, Blythe was not and she hurried her companions on after only a short time. A brisk wind was causing the temperature to feel at least twenty degrees colder than the thermometer readings. Since the inside exhibits were scattered over various portions of the zoo grounds, and since she was in no mood to tour the entire zoo in this bitter weather, she insisted that the twins choose one group of exhibits. After a minimum of discussion they decided on the Reptile and Monkey houses which were set close together on the hill above the seal pond.

Once inside the first building with its many glass-fronted habitat enclosures, Roger spent a few moments peering over the rail into the vegetation -lined pools built below floor level in the centre of the building. The alligators and crocodiles occupying these tropical-looking water-holes lay lazily, ignoring the spectators, giving the impression of inanimate objects in their frozen idleness. After which, he pursued his real interest which was that of identifying snakes which could be found in Wyoming.

'There's a rattlesnake,' he pointed out a lethargic brown body hanging in a loose coil from the fork of a dried tree branch to Tate. 'We have lots of those here in Missouri. Do you have any on your ranch?'

'Maybe a few,' the man acknowledged.

'That's why he has to wear those heavy boots,' Brian informed his brother. 'Snakes can't bite through them.'

Ignoring his brother, Roger continued his quest. A mosaic copperish creature moved slowly along the glass in front of him. 'What about copperheads? We have those here, too.'

'None that I know of.' Tate shook his head in a negative gesture. 'Of course, we do have our own variety of unusual creatures you will never find in any zoo.'

Immediately, both boys gave him their full attention.

'They are found only in the Sierra Madre Mountains outside of Dillon, Wyoming, or I guess I should say outside of what's left of Dillon. The place was one of the boom towns that rose and fell with the mining industry. Anyway, when it was a thriving community, a man by the name of Grant Jones operated the local newspaper, The Dillon Doublejack. He spent a lot of time in the Sierra Madre range and wrote about the unusual creatures and fauna he discovered there. For instance, there was the Cogly Woo. This was a six-legged animal with a sharp broad tail and when he was being chased he would stand himself up on the tip of that sturdy tail and whirl around so fast and so hard that he dug himself a hole to hide in. Then as he disappeared down the hole, the hole disappeared after him.'

'Whow! That would sure be neat to see,' Roger gasped with admiration.

'And then there was the One-Eyed Screaming Emu,' Tate continued with a grin. 'It was a challenge to even get a good look at this fellow. If anyone got too close he would swallow himself or herself up in one large gulp while casting a scoffing glance over his shoulder towards his pursuers.'

'Have you ever seen one of those One-Eyed Screaming things?' Brian questioned, as enthralled as his brother.

'No. But then I don't spend much time in the Sierra Madre Mountains,' Tate replied with a sad shake of his head.

'Or as much time with a bottle as Grant Jones did,' Blythe added under her breath.

As the boys moved on to view more normal creatures, Tate held back, remaining by Blythe's side. 'Drink can do strange things to a man's mind,' he agreed. Then his tone hardened as he added, 'Of course people today are more sophisticated and use drugs instead.'

'I wouldn't say it was more sophisticated. It's just faster, and in some cases more permanent.'

'And what would an innocent young widow like yourself know of such things?' There was an innuendo in the man's voice which caused her suddenly to feel defensive.

'Anyone who watches television or reads current news magazines knows about drugs, Mr Calihan,' she said icily.

'Please, call me Tate.' It was more of a command than a request. However, it was politely delivered, causing her to wonder if she had mistaken the earlier innuendo. Looking up at her companion, she could read nothing in his face. She did, however, receive the impression that he was used to issuing orders and having them obeyed.

'Hey, Mom, Tate. Come over here,' Brian called. 'We've found the Gaboon Viper. It's one of Mom's favourites.'

'And what is it about the Gaboon Viper that makes it so fascinating?' Tate inquired as they approached the twins.

'I guess it's that I always thought it was a joke,' she responded. 'I remember hearing a vaudeville routine once about the snake and I thought someone had made up the name. Besides, it's such a chunky little thing. It's hard to believe from its appearance that it's so very deadly.'

'Why should snakes be any different from other forms of life? Humans, for instance, are in many cases never what they seem.' Again she thought she detected an insinuation in his voice. However, when she glanced up at him warily, his expression contained only polite interest in the exhibit before them.

Attempting to shrug off the disturbing effect the man's presence had on her, she looked around for Roger who had wandered over to another exhibit. Approaching him, she discovered he was busily observing a couple of large hairy tarantulas moving sedately around their habitat on long jointed legs.

'George Marley had a whole lot of Missouri tarantulas he found down in the Ozarks on his vacation last summer. He even brought one in to class to show us. He wanted to take it out and let me hold it, but Mrs Wiley wouldn't let him.' There was regret and envy in Roger's voice while Blythe said a silent thank you to Mrs Wiley. 'He keeps them in a big aquarium in his basement.'

'His mother is a great deal braver than me,' she shuddered and, taking his hand, led him away from the objects of his admiration.

'They're not poisonous,' he persisted. 'At least, not the ones from Missouri.'

'Poisonous or not poisonous, they are not my idea of a pet.'

The boy's mouth puckered into a pout, but he dropped the subject as they left the building to brave the cold once more for the short walk to the Monkey house. Most of the exhibits in this building were in huge communal glass-fronted habitats. While the younger monkeys played, their antics entertaining the spectators, the adults sat stoically on the high rock backdrops, casting sage looks at the audience. In several cases, a young female with her new child would be sitting right up next to the glass front giving the impression that she was pointing out the humans to this newest addition of the monkey community, as if the humans were the show.

As they left this building, Blythe announced that it was time to go home, in spite of the protests raised by the twins who wanted to stop by the Children's Zoo, too. Promising them that they would return very soon, she firmly led them to the car. Back at home, she fixed soup and sandwiches for Tate and the boys, then, leaving them to eat in the kitchen, hurried to dress. The trip to the zoo had thrown her off schedule more than she had anticipated and being late was a luxury she could not afford this evening. She and George were dining with his mother and a few close family friends, and Mrs Lansky hated for her guests to be less than punctual. Regretting not having time to pull her hair back into a more conservative style, she ran the brush through it one last time and, grabbing her pearl necklace, headed into the kitchen to kiss the boys goodbye while trying to fasten the clasp.

To her relief, Ethel had arrived, but so had George and she did not like the way he was staring at Tate who sat nonchalantly at her kitchen table as if this was a completely natural situation. 'I'm sorry I'm late,' she apologised, giving George a quick greeting peck on the cheek as she passed him to lean over and kiss her sons. Then, directing her attention towards Ethel, she said, 'They are to watch no television.'

'No television!' the woman's face was more grieved than the boys. 'Not even Walt Disney?'

'Not even Walt Disney,' Blythe remained firm. 'They can colour or paint or play games, or you can read to them. They have to go to school tomorrow, so they should be in bed early, anyway.' A cry of exasperation followed this pronouncement as a fingernail broke on the unco-operative clasp of her necklace.

Tate was immediately out of his chair. 'Hold your hair out of the way,' he instructed.

She started to protest, but he had the necklace by this time and she didn't want to cause a scene. George was already glancing anxiously at his watch for the tenth time in the last minute. Tate fastened the clasp almost instantly, but did not release the light hold he had on the strand of pearls. Instead, he ran his thumbs lazily over the section of her neck below his hands, sending rivers of liquid fire radiating throughout her body. As if mesmerised by his touch she stood there, allowing him to continue.

'Blythe, let me fasten that catch.' George moved towards her. 'We're going to be late and you know how mother hates latecomers.'

'It's done,' Tate announced in a slow drawl, freeing her.

A faint blush reddened Blythe's cheeks as she turned to glare at the man who stood watching her with cynical amusement in his eyes, and thought how glad she would be when his lease was up and he was gone.

'Blythe!' George said her name impatiently.

Giving the boys each one more hug she left the kitchen. Tate Calihan was obviously a womaniser and a drifter and she had no intention of allowing his disturbing influence to ruin her relationship with George. She was in many ways very inexperienced, and she chose to believe that her reaction to Tate was due to this lack of experience rather than any real attraction towards the man.

'Who is that man, and why is he eating in your kitchen?' George demanded as they hurried through the livingroom.

'He's Tate Calihan.' She tried to sound casual.

'I know that.' He rewarded her with an exasperated look. 'Ethel introduced us. What I want to know is, why is he here?'

'I explained to you that I was helping Ethel because the boys gave her the chicken pox,' Blythe replied.

'I didn't realise that helping Ethel meant having strange men sitting around your kitchen like they belonged there.'

A shaft of apprehension shot through her. Tate did seem to belong. No he doesn't, she fought back. It just seemed that way because he was so overbearing. 'It's only for a couple more days,' she said in a soothing tone, giving George another quick kiss on the cheek before slipping into her coat. The hairs on the back of her neck began to prickle and, glancing over her shoulder, she saw Tate standing in the kitchen doorway watching them. Throwing him a defiant look, she exited, holding George's arm possessively.

Once in the car, the subject of Tate Calihan was forgotten as George said in an apologetic tone, 'I want to warn you about mother. She might be a bit testy tonight. I've told her in no uncertain terms that I plan to marry you.'

'Shouldn't you have asked me first?' Blythe suggested sharply.

Reaching over, he pulled her towards him. 'I was under the impression that the answer was already settled between us.'

'A girl likes to be asked.' She forced her voice to sound less hostile. She wasn't really angry with George. It was Tate. He had no right coming into her world and making her feel so . . . so . . . unsteady. Yes, that was the word—unsteady.

'Blythe. Blythe!' George repeated her name. 'I lost you there for a minute. You looked like you were a thousand miles away.'

'Not that far,' she confessed and with a monumental effort pushed her new neighbour to the far corners of her mind.

He had been right to warn her. Mrs Lansky was in top shape this evening. Her first approach was to chide Blythe for not spending Sunday evening with her children. 'I've always considered this particular evening of the week as one to be spent with family,' she proclaimed self-righteously, causing several of her guests to look questioningly in her direction since they too had been forced to leave their families in order to attend this dinner. Mrs Lansky was a wealthy woman and Blythe guessed that many of those present would have preferred to have been elsewhere had they not been worried about offending this woman who held so many purse strings.

To counter this attack, she launched into an overly copious description of her trip to the zoo with the twins, prudently leaving Tate Calihan out of the recitation.

Next, Mrs Lansky brought up the names of several women she hinted were ex-girl-friends of her son's, attempting to paint him as the playboy-type, and when that did not seem to work, she brought out her trump card. 'Sherril Cooper is back in town,' she informed her son with a meaningful look. Then turning to Blythe, elaborated, 'Sherril and George were an item for years. Almost from the time they were in diapers. Even as children they made the handsomest couple.'

George, as usual, simply ignored his mother's comments, neither refuting them nor acknowledging them, and Blythe knew he expected the same from her, but she couldn't, not entirely.

'I remember the Senior Prom as if it was only yesterday,' Mrs Lansky continued. 'Sherril was so lovely. She wore a pink chiffon and George wore a white tuxedo. She was only seventeen then and still had that innocent bloom of youth.' Pausing, as if to treasure this memory for a moment longer, she then noted in a cool tone, 'You had the twins when you were seventeen, didn't you?'

'Yes, I did,' Blythe confirmed, holding herself tightly in check.

'I tried to get Sherril to come tonight, but she made some feeble excuse. I have the distinct impression that she still has feelings for George, but she is too much of a lady to cause a scene.' This statement was directed pointedly towards her son who frowned sarcastically before returning to his conversation with the man on his left.

Again the woman turned her attention towards Blythe.

'There is one thing that surprises and puzzles me. George tells me that you and the twins are a sole family unit. That there is no extended family at all.'

'I have a few distant cousins scattered around the country, but I rarely see them, so I guess you could say we are a total unit.'

'Both your parents and your grandparents are dead?'

'Yes,' Blythe confirmed with an inward sigh. They had been over this ground before. 'My sister and I were raised by a maiden aunt.'

'And I believe you told me that they are both dead now, too.'

'Yes, they died together in a car crash.'

'But what about the twins' father? Surely he had some family.'

'No, as a matter of fact he didn't.' Blythe shook her head sadly. 'His parents were missionaries and died at the hands of savage natives in South America when he was still a baby. The only reason they did not kill him was because he had a birthmark in the shape of a star on his back, and they were afraid his spirit would come back to haunt them. They carried him to the church in the nearest town and left him there. The people there knew his parents and sent him back to the States to live with his grandparents. They, however, are also dead now.'

Mrs Lansky sat looking at her for a long moment following this story. It was obvious she didn't believe the tale, but was not willing to call her possible future daughter-in-law a liar in front of her son.

George shot Blythe a curious glance, but remained silent while Blythe wished she had kept her mouth shut. She could easily picture Mrs Lansky cornering her son later in the evening and cautioning him against a woman who would tell such outrageous stories. No doubt she would point out that such an improbable tale would only be told by a person who was covering up a very unsavoury past. Suddenly, Blythe became wary. What if she had overdone it this time and brought real trouble on herself? What if Mrs Lansky decided to hire a detective to find out the truth about the twins? The thought frightened her momentarily until she calmed down and thought it out fully. The woman couldn't discover anything important. Only Dr Harley knew the real facts, and he would never tell.

Thinking of Dr Harley and the past was a wearing experience, however, and she asked George to take her home early. She tried to talk him into simply dropping her off, but he insisted on seeing her in and, as she inserted the key in the lock, she knew he meant to talk to her about the story she had told his mother. The living-room was quiet and the lights were out. Guessing that Ethel was asleep on the couch, she ushered him into the kitchen.

'I know we agreed not to discuss your past,' he began in hushed tones. 'You told me that the boys' father's death was too painful for you to discuss, but sometimes the only way to get something like that out of your system is to talk about it. That story you told Mother this evening is only going to spark her into action. I know that look. So maybe you had better tell me the truth now.'

'I've never asked you to give me the details about your past,' she countered. 'I honestly thought we had an agreement.'

'There is nothing in my past to come between us, However, I cannot say the same about yours.' There was determination in his voice. 'I want a future with you, but I'm not certain we can have one with this man from your past standing between us. I know you loved him because you are not a precocious woman, and I am not sure I can live in his shadow without knowing something about that shadow.'

'Oh, George. You wouldn't be living in anyone's sha-dow.' She threw her arms around his neck. Tears, pent up from the undefinable strain she had been under the past couple of days, increased by his mother's harassment and now his probing, begged to be released. Yielding to her emotional side, she allowed the salty streams to flow freely. 'We were so young. It's not that I loved him more than I love you, but his death was so tragic. He was barely eighteen. Not even really a man yet.'

'It's all right. Calm down,' he soothed, patting her back as she sobbed on his shoulder. Blythe disliked doing this to the man. He hated tears. But it was the fastest way to get rid of him and she had no intention of telling him anything at this particular time. A chord of regret stirred within her. Earlier in her life, when she had still viewed the world in an idealised light, she had hoped to find a man she could freely confide in. But now she had been on her own far too long to cherish that illusion. Once they were married, she would probably have to tell him the whole story, and if he loved her as much as he professed, he would understand. Although she would feel more secure if he liked the boys a little better. It wasn't that he hadn't tried. They were partly to blame. If only they could have responded to him the way they responded to Tate Calihan.

'Now, you dry those tears,' he was saying, holding her away from him and dabbing at her watery cheeks. 'I'll be running along now, so you can get some rest. I'm sure you are simply tired.'

'I will,' she promised and, walking him through the darkened living-room, saw him out the front door with only a cursory kiss.

Leaning against the wooden barrier she breathed a sigh of relief mingled with guilt. George really did deserve to know the whole truth before he was legally bound to her, but she had protected the lie for so long it was difficult to trust anyone.

Suddenly, the stillness of the room was broken by lightly delivered applause followed by the switching on of the lamp near the large armchair. Startled, her breath caught in a muted gasp deep in her throat as Tate raised his lanky bulk from the chair and strode towards her. 'That's got to be one of the best performances I've seen to date. How do you do it? The tears, I mean.' His tone was cutting.

'None of your business,' she hissed back. 'And what are you doing here, anyway? Where's Ethel?'

'She had a television show she couldn't bear to miss, so I volunteered to read the boys to sleep.' He glanced at his watch. 'She's not due to return until eleven.'

Blythe knew it was now only ten-thirty and she felt a sense of danger sweep over her with the man's continued approach. Their first encounter came sharply into focus and again she felt the sensation of being cornered like a helpless prey.

'George certainly is good about getting you home early. Now if it had been me . . .' Here his voice trailed off as he reached her and his hands touched her. Moving caressingly up the line of her arms, they traversed her shoulders before capturing the taut cords of her neck in their velvet steel grip. Blythe stood motionless, unable to think, intimidated by his masculinity and the solidness of his presence. Slowly, tantalisingly, his lips descended on hers, their moist warmth playing over her mouth enticingly before hardening into a deeper assault.

She knew she should struggle and for a brief moment considered this possibility. But her body never responded and the battle never commenced. It was all so unreal. He had been so distant towards her, almost to the point of being hostile, and now he was kissing her with the passion of a lover. Her eyes closed slowly as she drifted into desire-drugged insanity. In her whole life no man had ever made her feel this way and, while the sensation was terrifying, it was also too exciting to resist.

Circling her arms around him, she clung to him for support. Then, as her lips parted in response to his persuasive demand, he suddenly pulled away from her. Holding her at arm's length he gazed mockingly down into her passion-darkened eyes. 'A woman like you needs a great deal more of a man's time than good old George is willing to spare.'

Humiliated, realising that he had been playing with her, Blythe wrenched free and edged away from him. 'Get out.' Her voice was a low threatening whisper as her hand moved behind her to grasp a paperweight on the desk near the door.

Tate was a man who had spent his life in a struggle for survival against a variety of foes, and the movement was not lost on him. Catching her wrist, the strength of his hold threatened to crush the bones. Releasing the paperweight, tears of pain glittered in her eyes, but still she stood her ground refusing to give in. They faced each other like two combatants poised for battle for what seemed like an eternity before Tate drew an angry breath and, without a further word, released her and left.

Sinking into the chair near the desk, she dissolved into tears. Blythe wasn't certain why she was crying. She told herself that it was because her wrist hurt, but down deep she suspected there was a more powerful reason. Finally, brushing the offending tears from her face, she pulled herself together and made her way into the kitchen. Mechanically, she began straightening up and preparing her percolator for the following morning. It was at this point that she remembered Tate Calihan's coffee. They hadn't purchased any during the day and she didn't want him darkening her threshold the next morning. In fact, the thought of fixing his breakfast made her stomach churn. Grabbing up her own can of coffee and retrieving a box of unopened cereal from the cabinet, she marched across the hall and pounded on his door.

He answered the summons, shirtless and bootless, glaring down on her with a dark intensity that would have cowed her if she had not been so angry.

'Wha—' he began, only to be silenced as she shoved the coffee can and box of cereal into his hands.

'Fix your own breakfast. You have milk and sugar, and I feel certain you can pour yourself a bowl of cereal.' She met his gaze with indignant fury.

When she turned to leave he caught her. This time his touch was gentler and there was a note of true remorse in his voice as he lifted the wrist he had held earlier. 'Damn,' he muttered under his breath, pulling her inside into the light to examine the swelling, purpling skin where his fingers had punished her flesh.

Blythe, too, looked with shock at her wrist. Her mind had been so preoccupied she had not examined it before.

'Sometimes I don't know my own strength,' he apologised tightly. 'Let me put some ice on that.'

'No thanks.' Pulling away from him, she escaped back into her own living-room, but she had not locked the door, and Tate followed.

'You have to put some ice on that. One of the bones might be broken.'

'Don't give yourself so much credit,' she shot back.

'Blythe, please.' His tone was harsh as if the words had cost him a great deal. 'I thought you were going to hit me with that paperweight.'

'I probably was,' she admitted. 'So don't feel so bad.'

'Now that we have that out of the way, let me put some

ice on your wrist.' The slighty arrogant tone had returned to his voice.

'I want to know what you meant by "a woman like me",' she demanded defensively, refusing to allow him to touch her.

'I only meant that you have a little more fire inside of you than George is possibly aware of.'

Instinctively, she knew he was lying and would have made an angry retort if Roger had not staggered sleepily out of his room at that moment.

Rubbing his eyes while yawning widely, he approached the two adults. 'What's going on? Is it morning already?'

'No, honey,' Blythe forced her voice to sound gentle. 'Go back to bed.'

'I thought you two were arguing,' he persisted, standing his ground.

'We were,' she admitted. 'I hurt my wrist and Tate was insisting on helping me, and I was telling him that I could take care of it myself.'

'You always say it never hurts to have a little help from a friend when I get hurt and you put the bandage on,' Roger reminded her.

'You're right. So if I agree to let him help me with my wrist, will you go back to bed?' she bargained.

'Sure. I know Tate will do a good job. Night.' With a sleepy, happy smile, the child disappeared into his bedroom.

Walking her into the kitchen, Tate took some ice from the refrigerator and, after wrapping it in a towel, ran it over the bruised and swelling wrist. 'I usually have a gentler touch with women,' he said in a curiously guarded tone as if he wanted to apologise again, but found it difficult.

'And I usually don't threaten people with paperweights,' she returned tightly. 'So let's just forget it. It's been a trying evening.'

'You seem to be able to handle George all right.' This was delivered matter-of-factly with no mockery attached.

'George isn't the problem. His mother is,' Blythe stated bluntly. 'She doesn't think I'm good enough for her precious son.'

'George obviously thinks you are good enough,' Tate pointed out.

'Maybe it's me. Maybe I don't think George is good enough for me.' There was a deep musing frown on her face. Running a hand through her hair, she looked up at the enigmatic man sitting beside her. 'Who are you, Tate Calihan?'

His eyes narrowed. 'What do you mean?'

'I'm not sure,' she confessed, focusing her gaze on his hands as they continued to manoeuvre the ice over her wrist. 'All I know is that you came into my, our, lives only yesterday and already the boys accept you like a long-lost friend, and I'm sitting here telling you things I haven't even admitted to myself until this very minute.'

'Maybe the boys see through my rough exterior and know that I'm putty underneath, and maybe you've needed a good listener for a long time simply to hear yourself think,' he suggested.

Blythe looked hard into the shuttered face before her with its deeply chiselled features and cold grey eyes. 'I don't think so. Personally, I think you're solid granite down to the very core of your being, and I'm tired and don't know what I'm talking about. So how about if you go home and we call it a night.'

Releasing her, he rose and emptied the ice from the towel into the sink. 'I'm sorry about the wrist.' His back was towards her as he delivered the apology.

'I know.' She still sensed that he did not like her, but she was also fair enough to believe that he really had not meant her any harm.

'And thanks,' he added from the doorway, this time turning to face her.

'For what?'

'For not telling the little guy how your wrist got hurt.'

Blythe nodded. She didn't know why, but she knew it meant a great deal to this cowboy that her son should not think badly of him.

# CHAPTER THREE

WHEN Tate arrived for dinner Monday evening, he brought a bouquet of roses. The boys exchanged conspiratorial smiles while Blythe hoped they weren't getting their hopes up that she and Tate might get together. He was the last man in the world she would consider for a lifetime partner. There was a coldness about him where she was concerned that caused her to reject him. Admittedly, she experienced a strong physical attraction towards him which both puzzled and angered her, and in spite of his snide attitude following his kiss on the previous evening, she was certain she had detected a certain tenseness about him that caused her to believe he was not totally immune to her. However, a physical attraction, no matter how intense, was worthless if the two people had no deep fondness for each other. A person's entire married life could not be spent in bed making love. Besides, it wouldn't be love it would be sheer animal lust. Shaking her head to clear out the muddled thoughts, she wondered why she even bothered to sort the situation out in her mind. It was a waste of time and energy.

After dinner when the twins wanted to challenge Tate to a game of Parcheesi, Blythe chased them off to their room to do homework. She was beginning to worry seriously about their growing attachment to this short-term neighbour.

The next evening she received proof that her concern was not unwarranted. After work, when she stopped by Ethel's place to collect her sons, the woman informed her that they had insisted on going up to visit Tate and he had let them stay. 'The twins are very fond of the man,' Ethel noted pointedly. 'Maybe you should open up a little and give him a chance. I know he's a little rough around the edges, but perfection can be boring.'

'George is certainly not perfect,' Blythe snapped back, then found herself wondering why she had not said that he wasn't boring instead.

'It's just that I hate to think of you with that Lansky woman for a mother-in-law. She's a tyrant if ever I saw one.'

Even though Blythe knew Ethel was right, she felt on the defensive. 'You really don't know what she is like. All you know is what the boys tell you, and they see her from a child's point of view.'

'That's not entirely true,' Ethel's eyes lit up with conspiratorial anger. 'She and that butler of hers, Brentwood, showed up at my door this morning. Said she wanted to inquire about my services. Can you believe that? She has a staff of twenty in that big mansion of hers and wants to inquire about my services?'

Blythe's face reddened.

'She wanted to pump me about you, that's what she wanted. Oh, she was very clever about it, but in the end what she wanted to know was if I knew anything about the boys' father and,' here Ethel's voice became decidedly hard, 'if you had other male friends besides her son.'

'What did you tell her?' Blythe tried to keep her voice calm in spite of the anger which boiled inside her at this blatant violation of her privacy by George's mother.

'Nothing. Well, not exactly nothing. I told her that all I knew was that the boys' father was dead and that you were as close to a saint as I have ever known.' A triumphant smile spread across Ethel's face.

'I'll bet that went over like a rubber crutch,' Blythe muttered, wishing for the hundredth time she had not made up that ridiculous story Sunday evening. Mrs Lansky could not learn anything important, but she could cause her some anxiety and raise a few very embarrassing questions.

'In case you're interested, I didn't get the job,' Ethel added with a laugh.

'Somehow, I guessed that.' Blythe forced a smile. 'And thank you.'

'Don't you think you should give Tate Calihan a try. He can be very charming. I bet if you relaxed around him, you would find yourself enjoying his company.'

'No.' Blythe's voice was firm. 'I'm looking for security, not adventure.'

'You're much too young to sound so matronly.' Ethel shook her head sadly. 'I hope you know what you are doing.'

'I do too.' Blythe confessed and, giving the woman a hug, went in search of her sons.

Upstairs, she found Brian and Roger sitting at Tate's dining-room table with their school work spread out around them.

'Tate's been helping us with our homework and we read him the books we brought home from the library today,' Brian announced with a happy grin as she entered.

'Yeah,' Roger chimed in. 'And after dinner he promised to teach me how to play checkers.'

'Both of us,' Brian corrected.

'If it's all right with your mother,' Tate stipulated.

'George is coming over,' she tried to explain, but the looks on the twins' faces warned her that George would meet with a difficult time this evening if he was the reason Tate wasn't allowed to come over. Out of the corner of her eye she was certain she caught a mischievous expression momentarily flit across the Wyomian's face. A sense of rebellion bubbled inside her. So he wanted to play games.

'I'll tell you what,' she smiled down on her sons, 'if it's all right with Tate, the two of you can come over here and he can teach you to play checkers. I'll come and get you when it's your bedtime. How does that sound?'

'Great!' both boys cried in unison, and she threw Tate a triumphant look.

A flash of anger showed in his eyes, then as they fell on her wrist hidden below the long sleeved sweater she wore, the shuttered look reappeared.

While she prepared dinner, Tate finished helping the boys with their homework in her living-room. She tried to wish it was George instead of the rough cowboy out there with her sons, but the thought of George brought the image of his mother into focus along with strong feelings of hostility.

'I thought I would help carry things out to the table,' Tate's voice broke into her angry contemplations.

'I can manage.' Her tone let him know that his presence was not welcome.

'You're still mad about the wrist.' His voice was factual, emotionless. 'Let me see how bad it is.'

'I'm not mad about the wrist.' She started to pull back from him, but he had her hand and was pulling up her sleeve before she could make good her escape. 'You see it's not badly hurt. I just have a lot of things on my mind.'

The swelling had vanished and there was only a mild discolouration. Satisfied that the harm had not been permanent, he released his hold and leaned against the counter watching her finish with the salad. 'Mrs Lansky on your mind?'

'Why would you ask that?' she shot back defensively.

'Ethel mentioned her visit.' There was mockery in his voice, as if he found all of this very amusing. 'She said the woman was checking up on you.'

'Ethel also claims that you can be charming, but I

haven't seen any evidence of that,' she threw back, then wondered why she had said such a thing and not merely ignored the man.

'Would you like me to be charming?' There was a challenge in his eyes as he shifted his weight towards her and his hand came up to trace the line of her jaw.

Moving away from his touch, she shoved the bowl of salad towards him. 'What I want is for you to put this on the table.'

For a moment he looked as though he was going to contest her request. Fire flashed in her eyes as she sturdied her resistance towards him. 'I have the impression that George sees you as docile. He's in for quite a shock, isn't he,' he mused with a derisive grin. Then, before she could find her voice to offer a retort, he exited.

Lucky for him that he had the salad, she thought hostilely while mentally picturing him with the bowl of lettuce dumped on his head.

Roger almost choked trying to gulp his dinner down quickly and Brian was not much better. For the first time since she could remember, they both turned down dessert. While she cut Tate a piece of cherry pie and poured him a cup of coffee, the boys collected the games and then stood impatiently by the door, watching him expectantly.

'Why don't I carry your coffee and pie over to your place,' she offered sweetly. The twins chorused the suggestion, forcing him to leave much sooner than he had obviously intended.

A few minutes later, as she straightened up the dinner dishes, a vindictive smile played on her lips. She had shown Tate Calihan that he wasn't the only one who could win when it came to manipulating others. Once the kitchen was clean, she went into the bedroom and pulled a pair of pale blue silk lounging pyjamas out of a bottom drawer. Laying them out on the bed she stood staring at them trying to make up her mind whether or not to wear them. They had been purchased during a fit of depression when she was questioning her own femininity, but had never been worn because they were not the type of sensible clothing one wears around children. Or George. The added stipulation popped into her mind and just as quickly she threw it out. It was Tate Calihan's influence. Just because George was less aggressive didn't make him less masculine. It simply proved that he respected her.

Returning her attention to the pyjamas, her eyes fell on the wide lace panel running down the outside of each trouser leg, beginning at the waist. Convincing herself that any indiscrete exposure of flesh would be hidden by the top which overlapped to the middle of her thighs, she slipped out of her sweater and skirt and into the soft flowing outfit. She had guessed correctly about the legs, but the top presented another problem. The basic body of this article of clothing was solid silk, however from barely above the bust line to the neck and including the sleeves, it was lace, causing her bra straps to show and producing a tacky appearance. Slipping off the offending piece of underclothing, she viewed herself in the mirror. Although the effect was very sexy and very appealing, she had never appeared braless in public before and could not help feeling somewhat uncomfortable. 'George isn't public,' she informed the image gazing dubiously back at her. 'You plan to marry the man. You shouldn't feel so shy in front of him.' Suddenly the question as to why she had decided to wear this outfit began to nag at the back of her mind. Was she testing herself, or George, and, if so, what was she testing?

With a shrug of her shoulders she went into the kitchen and opened a bottle of wine and cut some cheese. She had carried these refreshments out to the living-room and set them down on the coffee table when the door opened and Tate walked in.

'Roger needs . . .' He stopped in mid-sentence as his eyes travelled over her figure with a look of intense male appreciation. 'My, my. I believe I may have underestimated George.'

Blythe blushed red and had a tremendous urge to try to cover herself with her hands.

'Shall I have the boys sleep over at my place?' he suggested, approaching her with a dangerous glint in his eyes.

'No.' The nipples of her breasts hardened in expectation of his touch and she hated herself for reacting to this arrogant male.

'Silk . . .' His voice was low and harsh in tone as his hands circled her waist, crushing the delicate fabric to her skin. Slowly they moved upwards until they cupped the firm roundness of her breasts. 'Has a bedroom feel to it, don't you think?'

'Tate, stop it.' She meant for her voice to sound threatening, but instead the words came out as a plea. Her heart was pounding against her ribcage so violently it hurt.

'My God, woman.' He looked down on her contemptuously as he released her. 'You act like you're going to faint from fright. A person would think you had never been intimate with a man before.'

Not caring what he thought, she ran for the bedroom and, locking the door, changed quickly into a pair of slacks and a long sleeved turtle-necked sweater with a bra underneath.

'Couldn't you find the cards?' Roger's impatient voice sounded from the living-room.

'No, why don't you help me,' Tate responded, and she heard them move into the boys' room.

As she re-entered the living-room the man and boy

passed through on their way back to Tate's place. 'You look real nice, Mom,' Roger commented. 'Don't you think so, Tate?' There was a hopeful gleam in his eyes.

'Yes, but I wonder how she would look in a pair of silk lounging pyjamas,' the man mused, a mocking smile curling his lips.

'She'd look terrific in anything,' the child stated with a positive nod of his head.

'I believe you,' the cowboy returned, throwing Blythe an amused glance over his shoulder. 'Terrific.'

Fluffing up the pillows on the couch, she tried to work off her hostility towards the man who had moved in across the hall and had somehow become insidiously entangled in her life up to a point where she was not certain how to eradicate him. But eradicate him she would.

George's late arrival did not help her disposition either, even though he was full of apologies about his mother having a late dinner and then car trouble. 'And I wanted this evening to be special, too,' he said with a comfortable sigh as he sat down next to her on the couch and poured himself a glass of wine.

'Special?' she questioned, her tone still slightly hostile.

He studied her thoughtfully. 'Have a bad day?'

'You could say that,' she returned snappishly.

'Want to tell me about it?'

'No.' Sighing, she leaned over and kissed him lightly on the mouth. 'I'm sorry, George. Life has been a bit trying for me lately.'

'I know the boys can be difficult at times, especially Roger,' he offered sympathetically.

Straightening away from him, she glared at the startled man beside her. 'I've told you before never to say that.'

'Never say what?'

'Never say that Roger is especially difficult. He's no more difficult than Brian.'

'Now, Blythe.'

'Don't "now, Blythe" me, George. Neither one of the boys is all good or all bad. They both have their shortcomings and they are both extremely lovable. You simply have to get to know them.' Her tone was agitated. She was beginning to believe that he would never get to know the boys very well.

'Speaking of your twins, where are they?' he asked, hoping to change the tone of this conversation. He hated confrontations and really didn't understand what was happening to Blythe these days. Normally she was so even-tempered and level-headed.

'They're next door with Tate Calihan, playing checkers,' she answered, fighting to make her voice sound more natural and less emotional.

'Do you think it's a good idea to let them spend so much time with a stranger?' George frowned.

The volcano exploded. 'No. No, I don't! I think I should go over and get them right now.' And putting action to her words, she left the couch and headed for the door.

'Blythe, calm down,' he directed from the couch. 'I really don't understand what's got into you lately. You are over-reacting to every little thing and your judgment is not too good, either. That little story you told mother, for instance. Now she is threatening to hire detectives to check you out.'

'Detectives!' Blythe froze in her tracks. 'She can't do that. I won't have people snooping into my past. I would feel . . . violated. I could never feel anything but digust towards you if you allowed her to do such a thing.' She swallowed hard, hoping this tirade would have the desired effect, although she was not actually certain George had enough gumption to stand up to his mother.

'Don't worry, honey,' he assured her with an encouraging smile as she drew near to him. 'I won't let her do anything so foolish. I know that when the time is right, you will tell me everything.'

Again, she couldn't bring herself to confide in this man. 'Honestly, George there is nothing to tell. I was very young at the time. We both were.'

'We were all young once. I understand.' There was a slight edge to his voice as he glanced at his watch. 'I've got to run. The weather looks threatening and I promised Mother I wouldn't be long.' Pulling her towards him, he kissed her soundly.

Nothing! Blythe's mind cried in disappointment. Nothing! She got more of a charge out of being licked by the Smith's dog. It was Tate Calihan again. She couldn't deny that she found the man exciting and, next to him, George didn't stand a chance. It wasn't looks, either. If anything, George was the handsomer of the two. He had crystal clear blue eyes, pale blond hair and there was no lean hard look around his face like Tate had. George was fond of sports and even lifted weights to keep in shape, and his manners were excellent. He dressed well. There wasn't anything disagreeable about him. So why weren't there any fireworks when he kissed her? She hadn't noticed their absence before Tate came into her life because she had never believed that any man could affect her the way he did. Pulling her mind away from this disastrous train of thought, she refused to consider the most plausible reason for her reactions. She wanted security more than anything in this world and that was a commodity George could provide.

Cuddling up closer to him, she kissed him more soundly than she had ever kissed him before. Laughing deeply as he broke the contact after several minutes, he again glanced at his watch. 'I'm sorry I'm going to have to leave so early this evening, but I have a six o'clock call on the Racket Ball court tomorrow. It's business.'

Blythe blinked and found herself thinking that Tate would never have deserted an invitation like the one she had just delivered. He would have gone to bed early, but it wouldn't have been alone, nor because he wanted to rest up for a Racket Ball contest the following morning. Shocked by her own thoughts, she wondered what was happening to her. Hormones! that had to be the answer. Any minute now, she was certain she would start having hot flushes.

'Besides,' George was saying as he stood up and pulled her to her feet so that she could walk him to the door, 'you look overwrought. I think you need some rest.'

'You're right,' she agreed meekly. 'I'm not myself tonight.'

He kissed her lightly on the mouth. 'I'll pick you up at six on Friday. We'll make that our special night.'

'Friday. Fine.' She tried to sound expectant and hit the mark close enough that George did not notice the edge in her voice.

With one final peck on the cheek, he left her standing in the doorway following his descent down the stairs with a tired expression on her face. Her neat, orderly world was developing some weak spots and she did not like the feeling of foreboding that threatened to envelop her.

'Early night,' Tate noted from his doorway.

'He had an early business appointment tomorrow,' she returned, feigning indifference.

'You are one understanding woman. Anyone else might suspect him of having a late date.'

'You don't know George.' Her tone was more matter-of-fact than defensive.

'No, I admit, paragons are not my type.' It was obvious he was baiting her.

'No, they wouldn't be. You'd never fit in properly,' she shot back caustically. Then added, 'It's time for the boys to go to bed.'

'I'll bring them right over,' he promised with an amused smile.

Blythe had tucked the boys into bed and was straightening up the living-room when the thought struck her that Tate might be right about George having a late engagement. It was difficult to accept that any man could be as immune to a woman he professed to love as he was to her. Picking up the phone, she started to dial his number, then dropped the receiver back into the cradle. 'You're being ridiculous,' she scoffed at herself, but the urge was too great and before she realised what she was doing, she had again picked up the receiver and dialled George's number completely.

Brentwood answered and his, 'One moment, madam,' told her that George was at home and she suddenly felt exceedingly foolish.

To add to her embarrassment a knock sounded on her door at that precise moment, and she knew before asking who was on the other side. 'What do you want?' she demanded through the wooden barrier.

'The boys left their games,' came Tate's answer.

She considered telling him to leave them in the hall or keep them at his place, but already feeling foolish enough, she opened the door and motioned for him to enter. 'Leave them on the couch and go,' she instructed.

'Blythe, what's wrong?' George's voice sounded at that moment over the phone.

'Nothing's wrong. I just wanted to call.' She blushed as Tate looked towards her with a raised eyebrow.

'I don't mean to sound grumpy, but I was already in bed.'

Clenching her teeth she said, 'Well, you go right back to

bed and remember that I'm thinking about you and that I love you.'

'I know,' George responded with a satisfied laugh. 'Goodnight, Blythe.'

Her knuckles were white on the receiver as she moved it carefully into the cradle before releasing it.

'Checking up on your paragon?' Tate taunted.

'I had been a little edgy tonight and wanted to apologise,' she replied tightly. 'Normally, I'm a very easy going, amiable type of person.'

'I wonder what your problem could be,' he mused. 'Perhaps you have discovered that George isn't exciting enough for you. He's not going to change, you know.'

'I don't want him to change,' she snapped back. 'I think you are the problem.'

'Me?' His manner was shocked innocence.

'You bring out the worst in me.'

'Surely not the worst?' There was a quality in his tone that caught her attention and she stared hard at him.

'Get out!' she commanded suddenly unable to bear his presence any longer.

'Yes, ma'am,' he returned drily, and with long swift strides carried out her order.

The next two evenings she put her foot down and insisted that the boys spend their time with her without Tate. The man was there for dinner and she did nothing to prevent his spending time with them before she arrived home from work, reasoning that Ethel needed the rest or she would never recover, and Tate did do their homework with them. But after dinner she made it clear that he was to leave and he co-operated. The boys were also very good about obeying her demand. In fact they were almost too good and, finally, on Wednesday night as she tucked them into bed, she said, 'I appreciate the way you two haven't pestered me about Mr Calihan.'

'Tate explained to us about being good and going along with you. He says women have to be pampered to some extent or they get totally unmanageable,' Roger informed her with a happy grin. 'He sure is swell. Don't you think so, Mom?'

Blythe thought a lot of things about Mr Tate Calihan, but 'swell' wasn't one of them.

Brian shot Roger a warning look and Tate's name wasn't mentioned again.

The next morning she called the bank to say that she would be late for work and, after the boys had left for school, she knocked on Tate's door. Since their encounter on Sunday night she had not been fixing his breakfast as they had first agreed. However, she assumed he would be up since his morning paper was always missing when she left for work. When he didn't immediately answer, she knocked louder. Now that she had her courage up, she wasn't going to be put off.

'And to what do I owe this early-morning call?' he questioned, opening the door dressed only in a pair of faded blue jeans that hugged his muscular thighs like a second skin. Shaving cream covered half of his face and, as he moved his shoulders back in a stretching motion, his hard abdominal muscles tightened, and Blythe had a strong urge to reach out and touch the warm, taut flesh.

This disturbingly sensual reaction the man elicited agitated her, adding to the hostility that had been building since Roger's revelation. Glaring up at him, she said, 'I would like you to keep your nose out of my family's life from now on.' Then, turning on her heels, she stalked off to work.

When she returned home that evening it was to find her sons sitting glumly in Ethel's living-room staring at each other. 'They've been fighting ever since they arrived,' the woman informed her in an exasperated voice.

Blythe apologised and hoped that the boys' behaviour had not slowed Ethel's recovery.

As they walked up the stairs to their own home, Roger looked up at his mother dejectedly. 'Tate's decided that he doesn't like us any more. He says we can't come visit him after school.'

'I'm sure he just had business to conduct,' she offered, feeling like a heel.

'Will he still be coming to dinner?' Brian asked hopefully. 'I wanted to talk to him.'

'What about?' she asked.

'Men talk,' he replied seriously and would say no more.

'Why don't you do your homework,' she suggested with a sigh, 'while I get dinner started.' This business with Tate Calihan had made it more and more obvious that the boys needed male companionship. She knew George would be asking her to marry him on Friday and considered suggesting that they have a very short engagement. When the meal was ready and Tate still hadn't shown up, she made the boys sit down at the table and, admitting to herself that she had not handled the situation very well, went next door.

'Have you decided not to cook dinner for me either?' He greeted her with a frown when she showed up empty-handed.

'I thought you would be coming over to eat. The boys are expecting you.' The words cost her a great deal and did not come out in the friendliest tone.

'I figured you would want me to eat over here away from your family.' His voice was cold.

Running a hand through her hair, she looked down at the floor. 'I apologise. I didn't mean to sound quite so brutal.'

'Do you want to tell me what prompted the outburst?' It was more of a demand than a question.

'Fear. Fear prompted the outburst if you must know,' she answered honestly. 'I don't know if you are aware of how attached the boys have become to you or if you even care. But I can see it. They've become more hostile towards George. And what do I tell them when you leave? How do I explain to them that you're here one day and gone the next? Wyoming is a little far for you to commute to do their homework with them.'

Her forthrightness seemed to surprise him. 'I guess that is how you would see it from your point of view.'

What other point of view was there? Blythe shook her head at the man's obtuseness. 'Would you come over to dinner now?' she requested, not wanting to discuss this any further at the moment. 'And maybe later you and I can talk about ways to work you out of their lives a little more gently.'

Nodding his agreement, he followed her across the hall. Brian's face brightened considerably on Tate's arrival, but Roger continued to remain glum, a deep frown on his face. Blythe had never seen him so dejected before and it tore her apart inside. Tate, too, was obviously concerned. He made a special effort to talk to him, but the child remained reticent.

After dinner she invited Tate to stay, saying that she would make some popcorn later. Brian was estatic. Roger, however, excused himself and went to his room.

'Brian, what's going on with your brother?' she asked. It was obvious the child's problem was deeper than simply being refused a few hours of Tate's time.

'I don't know,' he shrugged, looking towards the closed bedroom door, a worried expression on his young face.

Blythe rapped gently on the door. There was no answer. Entering the room, she found Roger lying on his bed staring up at the ceiling. When she tried to talk to him, he answered only in monosyllables and finally she gave up.

Tate also tried talking to the child, but met with even less success.

'Maybe he's coming down with the flu and just feels grumpy,' she suggested, following the rancher's futile attempt. 'I'll keep a close eye on him.'

While Brian played checkers with Tate in the living-room, she cleaned up the kitchen. About the time she thought she was finished she spotted the boys' lunch boxes on the table near the front door. The thermoses had to be washed and the insides wiped out. Unlatching Roger's first, she raised the lid. The air in her lungs burst forth in a strangled scream as terror registered on her face at the sight of a monstrous blackish-brown spider sitting poised to jump. With arms that felt like jelly, she slammed the lid down, catching one of the furry appendages on the outside and the rest of the ugly creature on the inside. Brian and Tate were by her side in a moment. Holding the lid with one hand and her mouth with the other, she tried to stop shaking long enough to explain to them what had happened. However, all she could manage to do was to point to the furry leg dangling alongside the picture of Mickey Mouse.

Roger ran out of his bedroom. 'Mom, don't op—' The words died on his lips as he saw her pale face and Tate's angry scowl. With a burst of hysterical crying he fled back into his room.

At the sight of her son's disintegration into a flood of tears, Blythe's colour returned. Her concern for the child was stronger than any fear of spiders.

'You take care of him. I'll take care of the unwelcome guest,' Tate instructed.

'Get rid of the whole thing. I'll get him a new lunch box,' she choked out over her shoulder as she hurried towards the closed door and the crying child on the other side. Inside the room she found Roger, tears streaming down his cheeks, kneeling on his bed pummelling his pillow with tightly clenched fists. Drawing the hysterical child into her arms, she sat on the edge of his bed holding him securely to her and talking to him in soothing tones.

'I didn't mean to scare you, Mom,' he sobbed disjointedly as the hysteria subsided into normal crying. 'I was planning on Tate helping me find a jar or something to put Hairy in. Then I guess I forgot he was there.'

'Hairy is certainly a descriptive name for the thing.' She kissed the wet cheek nestled on her shoulder while an uncontrollable shudder shook her at the remembered sight of the creature. 'But I want you to promise me you won't ever bring anything like that into this house again without first discussing it with me.'

'I promise.' The words carried true conviction and Blythe breathed a little easier. Then, leaning back so that he could look up into her face, he added in a pleading tone, 'Mom, I'm not really bad, am I?'

'Of course you're not really bad. Mischievous, sometimes, but never really bad.' Brushing the wetness from his face with her hand, she tidied up his wayward hair.

'Old Mrs Carstairs in the next building is always telling her friends that I'm bad. She's always saying that you got one good 'en and one bad 'en.'

'Mrs Carstairs is an old woman. You mustn't take anything she says seriously. You are certainly not bad, and we both know that Brian isn't perfect.'

'You can say that again,' he muttered with a twisted half smile before his face became serious once again. 'But even your George says I'm a hellion. I heard him. I asked Ethel what a hellion was and she said it was someone with the devil in him. I know from Sunday School that the Devil is bad.'

'Being called a hellion is not all that uncommon for lots of little boys and some girls. And it doesn't mean you have the devil in you. Ethel simply didn't understand your question. Next time you tell her why you want to know the meaning of a word. Okay?'

The child nodded.

'As for George, if I remember correctly you had just chased his prize Russian wolfhound through his mother's favourite iris bed, and both you and the dog were a mess and the flowers were beyond redemption for that year.'

'I don't see why he got so upset over a few flowers and a dog.' The child stuck out his lip in protest of this injustice.

'I explained that at the time. The dog had been prepared for a show the next day and George had only brought him out for a moment. It takes a lot of care to get the animal's coat just right and the nails cleaned. That dog was probably better groomed than you've ever been and Mrs Lansky pays her gardeners a great deal of money to provide her with a garden that is the envy of her friends. It's important to her.' As Blythe rationalised for her son, a nagging anxiety crept into her thoughts. Just where would she and her sons fit into the Lansky household? Then she frowned at herself. Surely she and George would have a place of their own.

'Mrs Lansky doesn't like me, either,' Roger persisted. 'She told the butler she was sure I had bad blood.'

'There is nothing bad about your blood.' Blythe stared hard into his face to make her point strong. 'It's probably a lot better than hers.'

'But she doesn't like me!'

'She doesn't like me, either. But I don't let people like her bother me and you shouldn't either.'

The boy sat silently for a moment, then, burying his head against his mother's bosom, he said in a quiet little voice filled with pain, 'Tate doesn't like me, either.' The tears which had ceased to flow started afresh.

Looking up, Blythe saw the lanky rancher standing in

the doorway. He had obviously been there some time. 'That's not true,' she told her son. 'He likes you a lot.'

'Then why wouldn't he talk to me this afternoon? He just said he was busy and that we had to stay with Ethel.'

Blythe swallowed hard. 'Because I asked him not to spend so much time with you.'

'Why would you do that?' he demanded unbelievingly.

'Because I was beginning to worry that you two boys didn't understand that Tate wouldn't be around for ever. He'll be leaving at the end of the winter and you'll never see him again.'

'If he liked us, he'd come back.' Roger's chin started to quiver. 'He just doesn't like us.'

'That's not true,' Tate's voice sliced through the air as he approached them and lifted the crying child from his mother's embrace into his own strong arms. 'I do like you. I like you a lot.'

Again Blythe felt the affinity between the man and the boy.

'You were angry with me out there.' Roger indicated the living-room with a nod of his head. 'I could tell by how black your eyes got.'

'I admit I was angry then. You nearly scared your mother to death.' There was a gentleness in the man's voice that Blythe would never have believed him capable of possessing.

'You see, I am bad.' Roger hung his head.

'No. You didn't mean any harm. It was an accident.' Sitting down across from Blythe on Brian's bed, Tate settled Roger on his knee. 'Tell me. Do you think I'm a bad person?'

'No, you're special.' There was fathomless admiration in the child's eyes.

Brian had edged his way into the room by this time and, seeing his brother and Tate on his bed, crawled up and sat next to the man on the side opposite Roger. Reaching around, Tate lifted the newcomer on to his other knee. 'When I was your age and even a little older, I gave my mother a lot of trouble,' he confessed. 'I've always regretted it. She died before I could tell her how sorry I was. I wouldn't like to see the two of you following that example.'

Whereas the boys both looked stunned by this revelation, Blythe had no trouble at all picturing the man across from her as a young hellion.

'What could you do that was as bad as what I did?' Roger demanded, finding his voice.

'Well, once my mother caught me with a live rattlesnake. I was trying to milk its venom like I'd seen a man doing in a film we had seen in school.'

'What were you going to do with the venom?' Brian interrupted, a look of awe on his face.

'I hadn't decided that yet.'

'What'd she do?' Roger questioned, watching the man closely as if to discern the truth in what he was saying.

'She made me put the snake back in the bag and once she was sure I was safe, she fainted.' A look of dark remorse came over Tate's face. 'I thought I'd killed her. I wouldn't want you boys doing anything like that to your mother.'

'We won't. We promise.' Roger slid off of Tate's knee and, moving over to Blythe, gave her a hug. He was quickly followed by Brian.

She held them both to her for a long moment, then releasing them said, 'How about that popcorn now?'

'With butter,' Brian stressed.

'With butter,' she agreed with a smile.

A few minutes later she was in the kitchen starting the promised snack when Tate joined her. Leaning against the counter he watched her lazily. 'You were very straightforward with Roger. You could have lied about why I wouldn't spend time with him this afternoon, instead of admitting it was your fault.' His voice was level, neither friendly nor unfriendly.

'There was no reason to lie. Besides, small lies generally only lead to bigger ones and pretty soon a person is trapped in a lie so big there is no way out.' Feeling suddenly self-conscious and wishing she had not elaborated so fully, she changed the direction of the conversation. 'Where are your two tag-alongs?'

'They're playing a game of checkers. I am to play the winner,' he answered in a slow drawl, his eyes studying her closely.

'What about the loser?' She tried to concentrate on the popcorn and ignore the man's scrutiny.

'I play him second.'

The warmth he exhibited when the boys were present was gone and a hurtful feeling passed over Blythe. She found herself wanting to use Roger's words and accuse Tate of not liking her, but she knew that in her case he would only confirm that accusation and that was something she did not want to hear. Philosophically, she reminded herself that a person couldn't expect to be liked by everyone. But it didn't help much and she was forced to admit that it would have meant a great deal to her if the man had cared for her.

'I guess with the boys being twins you have a lot of trouble with people trying to categorise them into the good twin and the bad twin,' he broke into her thoughts.

'People have a tendency to do it with all children,' she replied with a deep sigh. 'They're always pointing out one child as being a hellion and another as being polite and reserved, or they say that one is artistic and the other one can't draw a straight line. What makes it so bad is that they start these generalisations when the child is so young that the child grows up living up or down to those expectations when the expectations might be all wrong. And, of course, twins, especially identical ones, lend themselves even more easily to this type of comparison. Although they look alike, they have different personalities and some people find it very easy to dump all the good qualities on one and all the bad qualities on the other.' The popcorn stopped popping and she poured it out into the bowl.

As she salted and buttered it, Tate asked in a voice with a curious edge to it, 'Aren't you going to ask me if it's true?'

'What's true?' she turned to face him. 'I don't need your confirmation about what I just said. Children are very sensitive to adult interpretations and what you label a child today could very possibly determine what he will become tomorrow.'

'No.' He shook his head. 'I know you're right about that. Aren't you going to ask me if the rattlesnake story is true?'

'Personally, the only part of that tale I questioned was when you said you only had one rattlesnake,' she commented pointedly.

Rewarding this observation with a low chuckle, he picked up the bowl of popcorn. 'There were four in the bag,' he grinned as he exited into the living-room.

# CHAPTER FOUR

'I SEE the Urban Cowboy is back,' George remarked as he eyed Tate's boot-covered feet. He had come to pick Blythe up for their Friday-night date and did not like the way this stranger made himself so much at home in her living-room.

'He's not from Urban,' Brian corrected. 'Tate's from Wyoming.'

'Mr Calihan has offered to stay with the boys this evening,' Blythe explained in a consoling tone. 'Ethel still isn't feeling like her old self yet.'

'And, besides, we still can't watch television until tomorrow and she hates to miss her Friday-night shows,' Roger added.

Sensing that George was tempted to make a comment, Blythe hoped that he wouldn't. Tonight was not the night to argue about punishments for the boys. She knew he would suggest that she should have relaxed her rule and insisted that Ethel stay with the boys, but what he didn't know was that Ethel would have come up with another excuse. The woman was determined to promote Tate Calihan, and no matter how hard Blythe tried to explain that Tate was not and would never be interested in her, Ethel continued to play matchmaker. Quickly, Blythe gave each of the boys a kiss. 'Be in bed by nine,' she instructed.

'Yes, Mom,' Brian promised, while Roger screwed up his mouth in a sign of protest, then, catching a warning look from Tate, nodded in agreement.

Blythe frowned and hoped George had missed the exchange. Then, as she turned to leave, Roger questioned loudly, 'Aren't you going to kiss Tate goodbye?'

Taking a deep breath to counteract the flush that threatened, she ignored George's scowl, and looking her son in the eye said, 'I don't kiss Mrs McFay goodbye, do I?'

'No, but Mrs McFay's a lady,' he replied with a challenging nod. 'And, besides, you always kiss George.' He made no effort to hide his distaste for this action.

Catching the darkly amused look in Tate's eyes, she wondered if he had planted that idea in Roger's head, but then decided that Roger had probably thought that one up on his own since Tate certainly wouldn't want a kiss from her. 'Goodnight,' she said with finality and, taking George's arm, exited.

'Where would he get the impression that you would even consider kissing that uncouth person,' George demanded as they walked to his car.

'Who knows where children get their ideas,' she rejoined in a voice that implied she was above listening to children and their prattle.

George threw her a dubious look, but allowed the subject to drop.

Over dinner, he asked Blythe to marry him and, after a moment's hesitation, she accepted. After which she spent the rest of the evening convincing herself that she could and would make George a wonderful wife or, at least, a good wife. She did not, however, follow through on her earlier inclination to ask him to make the engagement a short one. In fact, when he attempted to set a date, she suddenly began making excuses.

'After living in that huge mansion with your mother you will feel cramped moving in with me and the boys. I really think we should find a new place to live and get it ready for occupancy before we can determine a date,' she suggested.

He looked at her as if she had lost her mind. 'My family home is certainly big enough for all of us.'

'You mean you want me and the boys to move in with your mother.' She tried to keep the panic out of her voice.

'It is my home. My father left it to me on my mother's death and I do not intend to play musical houses.'

'It's just that I find it difficult to think of facing Brentwood every morning at breakfast,' she countered. There was a stubbornness about George that she had never noticed before.

'The man is merely a servant. You can learn to ignore him if his presence bothers you.' Following this pronouncement he returned his attention to his meal to indicate that the matter was closed.

Smiling weakly, Blythe went back to convincing herself that she was doing the right thing. She told herself that she was simply over-reacting; that George wasn't really stubborn or cold; that he was in a bad mood because of Tate's presence in her home. Tate Calihan. Everything in her life lately seemed to revert back to the man. His image haunted her the rest of the evening and it was almost anticlimactic to return home to find him in the livingroom reading. To make matters worse, his polite acceptance of her engagement rankled her and she realised that she had hoped he would show some sign of disappointment.

With her nerves already on edge she found herself fighting rising hysteria when George, following Tate's departure, developed an ardent mood. 'Don't you think,' he said, nuzzling her neck, 'that now that we are engaged it's about time you asked me to stay over?'

'Your mother has some very strong feeling against me and if you stayed over she would never let me hear the end of it,' Blythe reasoned. 'Not to mention the bad example it would be setting for the children.'

'You're right,' he agreed with a regretful sigh. 'I guess that's why I love you. You're so level-headed and rational. I'm glad to see you are back to your normal self again.'

She could almost see Tate mocking her. Once you're married, his cynical look said, you won't be able to put George off so easily. I don't intend to put him off then, she rebutted, wiping the sneering face from her mind.

'Do you want me to come over tomorrow and we'll tell the boys together?' George's voice drew her attention back to more immediate concerns.

'I have to clean tomorrow morning, both my place and Tate Calihan's. I'm still paying off that favour for Ethel,' she explained apologetically. Then realising that she was making excuses to put off the inevitable, she added, 'I'll tell them in the morning. Why don't you come over for lunch and we'll take the boys to the movies afterwards. Make it a real celebration.'

'Can I assume the cowboy won't be present,' George frowned.

'No, he won't be here,' she promised.

With one final long kiss, he said goodbye and left. Not even bothering to check to see if the kitchen needed to be straightened up, Blythe went to bed where she tossed and turned, waking several times to reassure herself that she was doing the right thing for herself and the boys.

The next morning she dragged herself out of bed to the sound of the Saturday morning cartoons playing loudly on the television set. A perfect backdrop for her future, she thought sarcastically, then shook off the unhappy mood rationalising that it was due to anxiety over how the boys were going to take the news of her impending marriage. Some time during one of her late-night self-confrontations she had decided to tell them first thing this morning. 'Before I lose my nerve,' she muttered, then scowled at her duplicity. This was all Tate's fault. If he hadn't come into her life she would have had no doubts about her decision and about the boys growing to like George once the marriage was a reality, but now she was uncertain.

Brushing her teeth a little longer than normal and fooling with her hair a few extra minutes, postponed her encounter with her sons for a while. Finally, facing the fact that she had two homes to clean, lunch to prepare and herself and the twins to make presentable before George appeared, she called a halt to her procrastination.

Walking into the living-room, she switched off the television and directed her sons to come and eat their breakfast in the kitchen.

'But you always let us eat in front of the television on Saturday,' Roger protested loudly.

'All right,' she agreed, already feeling like she had got off on a bad note. 'You can watch your cartoons while you eat, but first I have something I want to tell you and I know you will be happy and excited.' Two small expectant faces watched her closely. 'George has asked me to marry him and I have accepted. You boys have needed a father for a long time and now you will have one.'

'He doesn't even like us,' Roger protested. 'This kid Lloyd in my school has a stepfather who doesn't like him and he beats Lloyd all the time. He showed me his bruises once.'

'George will not beat you. He is always nice to you,' she replied firmly.

'That's right, now,' Brian chimed in with his usual air of authority, 'and that's because he wants to make a good impression on you. When you're married to him all of that will change.'

'And I think you a bit too young to be a qualified student of human nature,' she returned sharply, knowing she was fighting an uphill battle and feeling as if she was losing ground with each passing minute.

'What about Tate?' Roger interjected, changing the direction of his attack.

'Tate Calihan is not a consideration!'

'What's "not a consideration" mean?' he challenged.

'It means that I'm going to marry George and the two of you had better accept that fact. You'll have a beautiful house to live in and all kinds of new friends.' Blythe couldn't believe these words were coming out of her mouth. She had always reasoned with the boys in the past, but then she had never felt that her back was up against a wall like this before.

'I like my old friends,' Roger insisted.

'And we can't play in George's house,' Brian argued. 'He's always telling us to be careful and not to touch anything.'

'And his mother doesn't like us, either,' Roger argued. 'Who ever heard of having a grandmother who doesn't like you?'

'And the butler doesn't like us, either,' Brian interjected before Blythe could make an excuse for Mrs Lansky. 'He's always looking down his nose at us.'

'He looks down his nose at everyone. That's part of his job,' she countered. Then, before they could launch into any further tirades, she said, 'There will be no more discussion. I have made up my mind and you'll just have to make the best of it. We've always done all right together before, haven't we?'

'I guess so,' Brian admitted half-heartedly, unable to meet her eyes.

'But we don't need George,' Roger refused to give up the battle.

'Mom, why don't you give Tate a chance. You could learn to like him and he likes us a lot,' Brian pleaded, re-entering the fray.

'He doesn't like me.' Blythe's blunt delivery brought

such shocked looks to her sons' faces that she felt the need to smooth the remark. 'He doesn't like me the way a man likes a woman he wants to marry.'

Relieved smiles appeared. 'As soon as he gets to know you better, he'll want to marry you,' Brian assured her, while Roger nodded in the affirmative.

'As I was saying,' she pronounced each word with finality, 'I am marrying George and he will be here for lunch and the both of you will be nice to him. Understand!'

'Yes, ma'am.' Two small voices chorused while their eyes met in a conspiratorial commitment.

Breathing a resigned sigh, Blythe poured out their cereal and let them carry their breakfasts into the living-room. Immediately the sound of canned laughter filled the air.

Pouring herself a cup of coffee, she added two aspirins to her breakfast menu and reluctantly faced the fact that George would be in grave danger should he set foot in her home. The only solution to this dilemma was to ask Tate to talk to the boys. Surely the man would understand the problem his attachment to her sons had caused and would be willing to do this one little thing to rectify the situation.

However, one humiliating confrontation an hour was all she could handle, and facing Tate would be worse than facing the boys, so she decided to clean her house first. This also gave her time to practise several approaches between bouts of wondering how she had got herself into this ridiculous position of having to ask an almost total stranger to talk her sons into letting her marry the man of her choice. Periodically she convinced herself that requesting Tate's help would not be necessary, then she would catch the boys in a secret whisper and knew she had no choice.

Finishing her own housecleaning, she paused by the

couch on her way to the Forbes' place. 'I have to go next door and clean for Tate, now,' she told the boys. 'You two behave while I'm gone and if you need anything just come over and ask. But do not make nuisances of yourselves.'

Before her words were barely out they were both set to make a run for their bedroom and dress in preparation for finding several reasons to accompany her.

'No, you don't.' She stopped them. 'You two are going to stay here and watch your shows. I have work to do.'

'Oh, all right,' Brian agreed, while Roger poutingly returned his attention to Tarzan who was trying to save his elephants from extraterrestrial beings.

Tate was sitting in his living-room, wearing a white shirt and jeans with his stockinged feet propped up on the coffee table, reading a book. She could smell the fried bacon he had prepared for himself and knew that when she went into the kitchen she would find it neat, the pans washed and the dishes in the dishwasher. This again raised the question in her mind as to why he had originally requested that she prepare his breakfasts when it had been an unnecessary burden on her, and he knew it. But she didn't have time to pursue that avenue of grievance. She had a more pressing matter on her mind. 'Could I speak to you a moment?' Her voice sounded unusually stilted.

'Certainly, Blythe,' Tate replied sarcastically, looking up from his book. 'Do you suddenly feel the need of fatherly advice at this moment in your life?'

'No.' She was incited by his animosity and again considered not requesting his aid. Then she reminded herself that he was the source of the conflict. Swallowing her pride, she said, 'I need your help. You've seen fit to involve yourself with my sons and this has presented me with an acute problem.'

'Do you honestly believe I am the basis of your problem?'

'Your presence has presented the boys with what they view as an alternative to George,' she explained stiffly.

'Do you really think they would like George any better if I wasn't around?' He lifted an eyebrow in disbelief.

'I don't know,' she confessed. 'But I do think that they value your opinion and that if you spoke to them, they would accept him more easily. It would be for their own good.'

Putting down his book, he rose and moved towards her. Lifting her left hand in his, he examined the ring George had presented her with the evening before. 'I would be willing to bet this little trinket cost more than you earn in a year.'

'Don't judge me, Tate Calihan,' she warned.

'So you want me to convince the boys that George is the next best thing to bubble gum?' Dropping her hand, he captured her neck on either side, forcing her face upward.

'Don't, Tate,' she cautioned in a choked whisper as his head descended and his mobile, enticing mouth began to play disturbingly erotic games on her lips. Tears glistened in her eyes. Why couldn't George make her feel the way Tate did? Her insides burned with a need, a hunger for this man, as rivers of fire filled her veins.

Deserting her lips, he gazed down on to her face while she fought to maintain an indifferent façade. 'First you have to convince me.'

Before his lips could contact her again, she wrenched free. 'Stop it! Why can't you understand? George can give the boys the kind of start they need in life.'

'You seem to be doing all right. You own your own condominium, the boys have clothes to wear and you have food to eat.'

'I bought the condominium with the money from my aunt's insurance and the sale of her house. Now we live on what I make. What about when the boys want to go to college?'

'They're clever enough. They could get scholarships or, when they're in high school, I'm sure they won't mind having summer jobs. It would be good for them. You'll have to do better than that.' He caught her again, this time pulling her hard up against his long lean body. The sturdy muscles of his thighs burned their imprint into her while his musky scent played havoc with her senses.

Blythe could muster no defence against Tate as his mouth descended for a longer, more persuasive assault. A tiny tear of anguish escaped as sanity slipped away, deserting her to leave a whirlpool of frightening yet delicious sensations. Her lips parted to allow him possession as her hands moved over the warm, solid muscles of his back in a caressing motion.

Lifting her into his arms, he carried her towards the bedroom. Suddenly sanity returned. Desperately she struggled against Tate and against her own weakness, but he held her easily. The fear she had experienced on their first encounter encompassed her. Now her heart, which had been beating erratically with desire, pounded in response to her terror.

'Put me down,' she demanded as his lips left her mouth to travel over her neck and into the hollow between her breasts. He had her arms pinned securely as if he had anticipated a struggle and the only effect her squirming in his arms was having was to cause the buttons of her blouse to come open.

'I intend to,' he muttered caustically, as he dropped her unceremoniously on the bed and picked up his wallet from the top of the bureau. 'If you're willing to prostitute yourself for money, I'm willing to pay.' His tone was brutal.

'Damn you!' she screamed, rolling off the bed to stand

on the opposite side, using the wide expanse as a barrier between them. The flow of tears increased to run in rivers and drip off her jaw-line. 'It's not the money! I know I could work things out financially for myself and the boys. But I'm tired of working things out on my own. I know you can't understand that, being a man in a man's world. But since I was barely seventeen, I've had the total responsibility for the boys on my shoulders, and I'm tired. I want someone there to help me make the decisions. I want someone to hold me and tell me things will work out all right when times are rough. Maybe I'm being selfish, but I get so frightened sometimes and I wonder what will happen to the boys if something happens to me. I've made arrangements with Dr Harley, but he and his wife are getting old. How can I be sure they will find a really good family to raise them?'

'What about their father's family?' Tate stood motionless by the bureau watching her.

'They have no father. They only have me.' She stared at him defiantly, wiping at the offending tears with the backs of her hands.

Slowly, he returned the wallet to the top of the bureau. 'I think you are making a bad decision, but everyone has to learn from their own mistakes, I suppose. I'll speak to the boys.' Without any further comment he left the room.

Blythe collapsed on the edge of the bed and sat hugging herself until the trembling stopped. Who did Tate Calihan think he was, anyway? He didn't care about her. He was making a judgment as to what he perceived was best for the boys, and he had no right. He was a winter drifter. He had moved into the Forbes' place for a few months and had impressed her impressionable sons because he was a big, tough cowboy and cowboys are always special to kids. But he hadn't been there through the all night vigils when they were sick or comforted them when they were scared or simply put up with them when they were in one of their difficult moods. He didn't have the responsibility of feeding or clothing them or keeping a roof over their heads. He was nothing more than a stranger who had accidentally stumbled into their lives and the sooner he stumbled out the better.

It galled her that she had felt forced to ask him for his help with her sons and what irritated her even more was how, in one short week, he had become so much a part of their lives. Obviously the boys needed male companionship. She only regretted that George hadn't filled this need before Tate stepped in. Resting her chin in her hand, she faced the most important question—would George ever fill that need? He had been coming round for over a year now, and still the boys did not feel close to him. There was no natural affinity like the one they had towards Tate. Almost in an hysterical vein she considered asking George if he would don a pair of boots and a stetson to see if that would make a difference, but then decided that it wouldn't. 'Part of the problem is that he isn't honestly fond of the boys and they sense that,' she muttered aloud, admitting a truth she had tried to bury. But surely that would change once they were married and he got to know them better. They were very good children.

Suddenly remembering that Tate would be returning, she rose and began cleaning rapidly. She had no desire to spend any more time in the man's immediate presence than was absolutely necessary. Only the vacuuming was left when he walked in and, with only a cursory nod in her direction, sat down and resumed reading his book. Her pride refused to allow her to ask him how his talk with the boys had gone.

Working around him, she found his presence disruptive. The vivid memory of his touch taunted her and she chided herself for letting him bother her. He was arrogant, self-righteous and cruel. He had proved that by his little game this morning, making his point with vulgar brutality. Finally finished, she paused with her hand on the doorknob. 'Ethel will make your dinner tonight.'

But before she could make her exit complete, he asked, 'What about breakfast tomorrow?'

'What about it?' she snapped back.

'I did talk to the boys.' There was hint of blackmail in his manner. 'And I enjoyed our little arrangement last Sunday. I'm curious to see if Roger and Brian can make it through another whole sermon without picking up a hymnal and playing with it.' There was a wistfully amused expression on the man's face that surprised her and in answer to the quizzical look she shot him, he added, 'I was young once.'

'I thought maybe you were simply born a full grown egotist,' she returned drily. 'But I guess I do owe you something for talking to the boys, provided your little session worked and they are more amiable towards George.'

'Speaking of George,' the cynical look was back in the man's eyes. 'Are you sure he won't mind my accompanying all of you?'

'He won't be here. He and his mother are very active members of their own church, and he teaches Sunday School.'

'I'm surprised you and the boys aren't going to attend there, and get to know his friends better.'

'I know his friends.' Blythe couldn't control the slight edge in her voice. George's close friends had all been born to money and social position. They weren't exactly snobs, but she had never felt comfortable with them and when she was around them she often found herself wondering why George had picked her. Catching the mocking gleam in Tate's eyes, she continued rapidly, 'Besides, the boys are used to their own Sunday School.'

'And you don't want to miss Miss Taylor's most engrossing lecture on the significance of Ruth's dedication in the modern world,' he finished.

'What I wouldn't want to miss,' she countered sarcastically, 'is watching her try to keep her mind on her subject while flirting with you and making a fool of herself in front of everyone.'

'You sound like a jealous girl-friend,' he taunted.

'Jealous!? Jealous of a woman who is taken in by a cool smile from beneath a stetson and feet encased in a pair of cowboy boots!'

The grey eyes watching her darkened dangerously for a brief moment before again becoming shuttered. Blythe flushed slightly recalling her own recent susceptibility to this Wyomian's very masculine charms. Expecting him to make a snide remark in reference to their earlier encounter, she was surprised when, instead, he said, 'You're a good-looking woman and I noticed that several of the men in the class paid you quite a bit of attention.'

'Most of the men in that class are married,' she pointed out dubiously, not trusting him to have merely been making a complimentary statement. With their history that would have been too out of character.

'But not all of them. Why settle for George when there are others available?' It was a challenge.

'You would be surprised at how many men shy away from the responsibility of instant fatherhood.' Her voice was liquid ice.

'Perhaps, but what I am more surprised about at this particular moment is that you didn't proclaim your love for the man. Does he know you are only marrying him for the sake of your children?'

'I do love George!'

'No, you don't. And I have decided to make you an alternative proposal to help you out of this dilemma. You can marry me.'

'Marry you?' The words came out incredulously. 'You don't even like me.'

'However, I am very attached to the boys and they are attached to me. Therefore, I would be fifty per cent better off than George. I would at least have half of the bargain. He doesn't have any.' His face and tone were black with cynicism.

'You . . . you . . .' Blythe stammered, then, turning on her heels, she left the room, hot tears burning behind her eyes.

Back in her own home, she found both boys neatly dressed and their room cleaned up.

'Tate said it's always a good idea to make a favourable impression on people who are important in your life,' Brian explained, obviously parroting Tate Calihan's words as she stared at them in amazement.

'And don't worry, Mom,' Roger assured her. 'We will be gentlemen at all times.'

She didn't believe what she was hearing. She hated being grateful to the infuriating, arrogant, plus several other adjectives not normally in her vocabulary, man next door, but she had to admit that he had worked a miracle.

George, too, was pleasantly shocked upon his arrival. 'I suppose it was the fact that I asked you to marry me, thereby proving to them that I was sincere in my regard for you, that has changed their attitude towards me,' he whispered in an aside to her after the two boys had graciously accepted the gifts he had brought them and congratulated him on his engagement to their mother.

Blythe merely smiled and waited for the moment of reckoning. But it never came. All afternoon her sons were as close to angels as they had ever been in their entire lives.

They were polite during lunch and actually asked to have things passed to them rather than standing on their chairs and reaching. In the movies neither one spilled his pop-corn or soda on George, themselves or anyone else. After-wards, they went out for a pizza and when they finally arrived back at home, the boys went in to take their baths and get dressed for bed without being told. George was beaming and couldn't say enough about how tremendous the twins were, while Blythe felt exhausted from waiting for the devilry to burst forth ten times worse than normal.

Pulling her down beside him on the couch, George began to nuzzle her neck. It was one of his favourite pastimes and was begining to grate on her nerves. 'Why don't I make us some coffee,' she suggested, pulling away, certain that her reaction was due merely to nerves and that tomorrow she would again be happy to have him play with her neck.

'I don't feel like having anything to drink,' he mur-mured into her ear.

His warm breath caused a shudder to sweep over her as if she had been chilled by a cold wind. Maybe, after waiting all this time, I'm frigid!—the thought shot through Blythe's mind. But then she recalled her reaction to Tate. Of course, with him it had only been a stand-off game. She would be marrying George and there would be no stand-offs.

Roger interrupted this distressing train of thought. 'Will you play me a game of checkers?' he requested of George, bringing the board out and plopping down on a hassock across the coffee table from the couple on the couch.

With a mild sigh, George smiled patronisingly at the child. 'Of course, son,' he said, and although Blythe caught the flash of hostility in Roger's eyes, the child remained complacent and polite.

On her way into the kitchen she wondered what Tate could have told them to cause them to behave so well. Whatever it was, she chose not to worry about it. George and the boys were having a pleasant time together and she felt certain that getting to know one another without the barrier of animosity that had been present before would lead to a peaceful, solid relationship.

When she returned to the living-room with drinks for everyone, she found Brian perched next to his brother facing George across the checker board and demanding to play next. For an hour the boys kept their future father occupied until he finally suggested that it was getting late and they needed to go to bed. Blythe agreed. It was already nine and they had to be up early for church the next morning.

'But we want to visit with George,' they both protested.

'You'll both be spending the rest of your lives in my company,' he reminded them with a pleased laugh.

'George is right. Now off to bed with you two,' Blythe commanded.

Reluctantly, the boys obeyed. Reaching their bedroom door, they turned to say goodnight. 'And don't you stay up too much longer either, Mother,' Brian instructed, throwing Roger a cautionary glance. 'Remember we do have to get up early for church tomorrow.'

'They are very protective,' George noted with approval. 'I like that. A boy should look after his mother.' Despite his words, there was a rebellious edge in his voice as if he wasn't totally convinced of what he was saying.

A sense of guilt swept over Blythe as she wondered how much of a conflict her association with George had caused between him and his mother. Then she reminded herself that he was a grown man and should be making decisions about his life for himself. Covering a yawn with her hand, she said, 'They are right. I do have to be up early and I have cleaned two homes today, not to mention all the running around we did this afternoon.'

'Of course,' George agreed, rising and pulling her to her feet for one last long kiss.

He kissed very nicely, she noted almost clinically as the man's lips played over her mouth and his hands caressed her expertly. There was no doubt in her mind that he would make love with as great an expertise. However, she could not help wishing that there was a bit more passion in him. Tate Calihan's image suddenly filled her mind and with an angry mental retort to herself she wrapped her arms more tightly around George and returned his kiss with more than her usual amount of ardour.

'Maybe I should stay a little longer,' he murmured as their lips parted.

'No, I think you had better leave now.' She schooled her voice to hint that if he stayed, she wouldn't be able to control herself, then helping him on with his coat allowed one final kiss before pushing him out the door.

From the doorway she watched him descend the stairs. She was still standing there, chewing on her thumbnail, an anxious expression on her face, when Tate's door opened.

Leaning against his door-frame with easy nonchalance, he asked, 'How did it go?'

'It went fine,' she replied quietly, wondering why she felt like crying.

'That's good.' His expression was shuttered as usual, causing her to think that he would have made an expert gunfighter in the Old West. His opponents would never have been able to guess his moves or what he was thinking.

'I thought you and George might have had a quarrel. He did leave very early for a man in love.'

'No. I asked him to leave because I was tired. It's been a

long day.' She continued to stare down the empty stair-case, her mouth a tight, straight line.

'Once you are married, I suspect there will be a lot of long nights.' There was a lurid, challenging quality in his tone and without giving his remark the dignity of an answer, she swung into her living-room and slammed the door. She hated him for being so callous and so crude, but mostly she hated him for voicing the thought that had been preying on her mind since George's departure.

Lying in bed later, she tried to sort out the situation. First she admitted to herself, for the first time without reservation, that she was not in love with George. However, she was determined to make him a good wife and that was what was important. Maybe there would be more duty than passion in their bed, but that was the way it had been in the past when marriages were arranged and those unions had worked out a great deal better than many modern marriages. She could almost hear Tate's voice mocking her, but she ignored him and fell asleep assuring herself that she would make George a wonderful wife, and he would be a good father to the boys.

# CHAPTER FIVE

HAVING forgotten to set her alarm, coupled with a restless night, Blythe overslept on Sunday morning.

'Wake up, Mom,' Roger's and Brian's cheerful voices roused her in unison.

Yawning and stretching, she opened her eyes slowly to find her sons beaming down on her. Glancing at the clock, she practically jumped out of bed. 'I'm late. You should have woken me soon,' she yawned. 'Have you made your beds?'

'Yes,' Brian assured her.

'And Tate's in the kitchen. He fixed us breakfast,' Roger added.

'Fixed breakfast!' Blythe was into her robe and on her way into the kitchen before the words were out of her mouth.

'He made pancakes,' Roger elaborated, 'and they were great.' Then, in an obvious concession to her feelings, added, 'but not as great as yours.'

'We were supposed to get dressed as soon as we woke you,' Brian finished as the two boys followed in her wake.

'I think that is an excellent idea. Go get dressed.' Her tone was stern and, although they looked at one another dubiously, the twins changed direction and went into their bedroom.

'Why didn't you have the boys wake me when you arrived?' she demanded, bursting into the kitchen to find Tate sitting at the table reading the Sunday paper and drinking coffee.

'Whatever happened to "Good Morning"?' he questioned, as if he was doing nothing out of the ordinary and it was she who was being unreasonable.

'Whatever happened to my nice, organised, peaceful existence?' she snapped back.

A half smile curled one side of his mouth. 'I should think you would be grateful to me for allowing you to sleep a little longer. However, perhaps I did let you sleep longer than I should have. You'll have to hurry to be ready for church on time.'

Storming out of the kitchen, she went back to her room where she muttered to herself continuously while she dressed. Tate Calihan's unorthodox intrusion into her home was inexcusable. Her day was now totally off-schedule and she would probably spend the rest of it feeling as though she was trying to catch up with herself. There would barely be time to put the ham in the oven before they left for church, and there would be no time to straighten up the kitchen.

However, when she did return to the room in question, it was to find that Tate had cleared off the table, wiped off the counter and put the dirty dishes in the dishwasher. For some inexplicable reason this irked her even more than leaving the room in a mess, but she held her tongue.

'Tate learned to cook on the open range over a campfire,' Roger informed her in a tone that spoke of admiration for the lanky cowboy, as they put on their coats.

'My home is not his range and I hope he keeps that in mind for the future.' She glared at the man, the hostility in her eyes accentuating her words.

The boys turned worried faces towards Tate, who merely tipped his hat in salute and, in an unperturbed voice, said, 'Yes, ma'am.'

Taking their cue from him, the twins relaxed somewhat and spent the walk to church describing to him, in minute detail, the plot of the movie they had seen on the previous afternoon.

Removing her coat and gloves on reaching the church, Blythe noticed that she had forgotten to put her engagement ring back on after washing her face. Picturing it lying on her dresser, she recalled planning to go back for it after putting the ham in the oven, but her anger towards Tate had erased that thought from her mind.

Glancing up, she discovered Tate observing her naked finger. 'A curious omission,' he noted drily.

'Maybe it's just as well,' she returned nonchalantly, refusing to allow him the upper hand. 'It would be difficult to explain being engaged to one man and attending church with another. Someone might even get the impression that it was you I was engaged to.'

'Yes, they might.' There was a blackness in his expression that caused Blythe to feel as if she had been insulted.

Clenching her teeth, she gathered the boys together and walked them down to their Sunday School room. Remaining outwardly polite, she chose not to speak to Tate for the rest of the morning, but this manoeuvre did not win her revenge because he said nothing to her which she could ignore. For a moment, when Sara Taylor cornered him following their Sunday School class, she again considered mentioning that he was a man alone, but a warning look from those grey eyes stopped her. She still needed the boys' co-operation—she was counting on this neutral time between them and George to build a bond of friendship.

Tate was again eating Sunday dinner with them after church. Ethel had asked Blythe to do this for her and the boys expected it. Having no intention of getting them into a bad mood since this afternoon was going to prove a great deal more difficult than yesterday because they would be spending it in the company of George's mother, she forced a smile and tried to act less antagonistic towards her unwelcome guest. Carrying the ham out and setting it on the table, she called the boys and Tate in to eat. 'George will be here by two,' she addressed this remark to Tate in such a manner as to let him know that she expected him to be gone before George's arrival.

He nodded to indicate he had got the message.

Roger screwed up his face in a look of distaste. 'Is he going to sit around all afternoon and kiss your neck?'

She flushed in embarrassment. 'He doesn't do that all of the time.' To add to her discomfort, Tate was standing behind her chair waiting for her to be seated. 'I don't need your help,' she glared at him, wanting as much distance between herself and this man as possible.

'The best way for the boys to learn good manners is to observe them being practised.'

The reasonableness of his tone infuriated her further. However, having no valid argument to offer, she seated herself and allowed him to help her with her chair.

'I'll bet Tate doesn't go around kissing women's necks,' Roger persisted, watching the manoeuvre.

'You mean like this?' Moving Blythe's hair to one side, the cowboy lightly ran his lips along a sensitive cord of her neck.

'Yeah,' Roger grimaced.

'Never,' Tate responded with a laugh as he straightened and walked around to his side of the table while Blythe sat clutching the arm of her chair and fighting back the burning sensation his touch had evoked.

'It looked different when you did it,' Brian mused. 'And Mom looked different, too.'

'Excuse me.' Blythe left the table and walked swiftly to her room where she found George's ring, and shoved it back on to her finger.

By the time George arrived, Tate was gone and the boys had chosen a few toys to take with them to the Lansky house. As they came to a halt in front of the three-storey mansion with its huge columns and marble steps, Blythe made up her mind once again to suggest to George that they purchase a place of their own, at least, in the beginning. Then, noticing a small red sports car parked in the drive, she said, 'It looks as if you have company.'

'That's Sherril's car.' There was an uneasy edge to George's voice, causing her to look at him more closely.

'Sherril Cooper?' she questioned, watching his jaw harden.

'Yes. She's an old family friend.'

'One of your old flames, according to your mother.'

'Mother exaggerates.' Leaning over he kissed her cheek. 'I hope you're not going to play the jealous fiancée.'

'No,' she promised, now very much interested in meeting the woman in question.

Ushering the boys into the house, they found Mrs Lansky in the conservatory with a slender blonde-haired woman whom Blythe judged to be closer to George's thirty-two years than to her own twenty-four.

'I've been asking Sherril what to do about my fish,' Mrs Lansky said, indicating the golden carp swimming around in the pool at the base of the large fountain occupying a corner of the room. 'They don't seem to be as active as they used to be, but she says they look fine to her and she should know. She's a marine biologist.' Then, directing her attention to Sherril, the woman added in a condescending note, 'Blythe is a teller in one of our banks.'

'Then she is more talented than I,' the woman responded, extending her hand in greeting. 'Because I cannot balance my cheque-book no matter how hard I try.'

'You, my dear, don't have to,' Mrs Lansky pointed out with a superior smile. 'Your accountant does that.'

Sherril threw Blythe a sympathetic smile as if to say she knew George's mother could be difficult.

'Sherril is quite the scientist,' George broke his silence. 'She is so devoted to her career that we haven't seen her for nearly ten years, except in passing during her holidays. I'm surprised she found time to inspect our fish this trip.' There was an acidness in George's tone that startled Blythe, and before she recovered from this display of uncharacteristic behaviour, he turned his full attention towards the blonde woman and said in a tone that could only be described as challenging, 'How long do you plan to remain in town this time?'

'Only two weeks,' the woman responded, avoiding his gaze. Then, attempting to change the direction of the conversation, she turned towards the twins. 'And who are these two handsome young men?'

'They are my sons,' Blythe replied, going on to introduce the boys while watching George and the woman closely. There was something between them and although George would like people to believe it was hate, Blythe suspected that it was something quite different.

'Most people can't tell us apart,' Roger said as he shook the woman's hand. 'Except Mom dresses us differently. She says it's important for each person to be themselves and not only half of a pair.'

'And she's right,' Sherril agreed. As she turned back towards Blythe, her eyes fell on the ring and she paled visibly.

'In addition to being a teller at one of our banks, Blythe is also my fiancée.' George's manner made Blythe feel as if she was being used as a weapon and she shifted uncomfortably.

'Congratulations,' Sherril replied, meeting his eyes for the first time. But the contact held only for a moment before she swung towards Mrs Lansky and extended her hand in salutation. 'I really must be on my way. My parents are expecting me.' Bidding Blythe and the boys a hasty goodbye, she retreated in spite of Mrs Lansky's strenuous objections.

'I recall a time when you objected to Sherril,' George remarked coolly to his mother after the woman was gone.

'People change. She's grown into a very cultured lady,' she replied.

Frowning, he led the boys to the games room, leaving Blythe to spend the rest of the afternoon fending off his mother's continued probing into her past and the boys' paternity. The more the woman probed, the more agitated Blythe became and, by the time they returned home, she felt drained and was forced to view the afternoon as a complete disaster.

George didn't help her peace of mind either. When she again broached the subject of finding a home of their own, he continued to be adamant about remaining at his present residence. In the end she was left with the impression that he was testing her, which added a final sour note to an already bitter day.

The next morning she did not wear her ring to work. In order to avoid friction between herself and the other employees, she had convinced George early in their relationship that they should keep their liaison private. Now she insisted on maintaining this private profile until their plans were more concrete, pointing out that she was still only a lowly teller and he would one day inherit the entire banking complex. At the present time he owned forty per cent while his mother controlled the other sixty per cent, and the significance of the arrangement manifested itself that Monday morning.

Calling her into his office, George claimed a welcoming kiss before explaining that his mother had decided that it was time for him to move into the executive offices in the bank's headquarters.

'Since this means I won't be seeing you during the day, I will be coming over to your home each evening,' he said as he cleaned out his desk. 'Mother is not going to separate us.'

There had been an inflection in his voice that had bothered Blythe, and as she mused over their conversation during the rest of the day, it occurred to her that he might not be as much in love with her as he purported. The possibility that he viewed his commitment to her as a stand against his mother and was determined to maintain this position, no matter what the consequences, could not be denied. If that was the case, she did not believe it was a conscious action on his part. Nevertheless, it could be very destructive to all of them if that was the basis of their marriage. The more she considered his reaction to Sherril Cooper, the more convinced she became that she had to find out the truth before this engagement went any further.

Arriving home, she found the boys as usual in Tate's living-room. Ethel was there, too, cooking dinner.

'Ethel is making enough for all of us,' Roger said. 'We can stay for dinner, can't we?'

'Sure,' Blythe agreed absently, causing Tate to look up at her curiously. Then, in a more positive tone, she added, 'But after dinner we have to go home. George is coming over.'

'Tate promised to play Parcheesi with us tonight,' Roger protested.

'Only if it was all right with your mother,' the man interjected.

'If you play over here, then it's all right with me,' Blythe agreed, surprising everyone. The boys were delighted. However, Tate seemed less than pleased.

'Decided you want some time alone with George?' he questioned drily when the boys went into the bathroom to wash their hands for dinner.

'As a matter of fact, I do,' she replied levelly.

'I thought the idea was for him to get to know the boys better to see how good a father he would be.'

'I've decided that I want to get to know him better to see how good a husband he will be.'

His eyes flashed black. 'What if he doesn't come up to your standards?'

Realising he had misinterpreted her intentions, she met his gaze with equal hostility. 'There are more aspects to a man than his bedroom capabilities that determine if he will make a good husband.'

'And am I to believe it is these other aspects you are so concerned about?'

'You, Mr Calihan, may believe whatever you wish.' Refusing to spar with the man any longer she went into the kitchen to see if Ethel could use any help.

George wasn't the least bit disappointed with the boys' absence and immediately pulled Blythe down on the couch beside him. 'Why don't we thwart Mother's plans completely and run away and get married this weekend?' he suggested after an initial prolonged kiss. 'I understand elopements are considered very romantic.'

'Running away with two seven-year-old boys isn't romantic, it's insane.' She tried to keep her tone light. 'Besides, I've been thinking that I want a big wedding. We'll invite all of your friends and throw a real bash.'

'I thought you preferred more intimate gatherings.' He seemed confused and mildly displeased by this sudden change of attitude on her part. 'You told me you were no good at planning large functions.'

'I know, but I've changed my mind. That's a woman's

prerogative. I was thinking that I could ask that friend of yours, Sherril, for some pointers.'

'Leave Sherril out of this.' It was a command.

Looking at him narrowly, she said, 'I think you should tell me about Sherril.'

'There's nothing to tell. We went together when we were young and then she went away to devote her life to science.' His jaw tightened and he stared at an empty space on the wall.

'You were in love with her,' Blythe accused, attempting to get at the truth.

'It was only an infatuation. We were very young. You know how young-love can be.'

The barb in his last sentence caught Blythe unawares. It was out of character for him and she decided to change the direction of the conversation before their exchange became hostile. 'I'll tell you what. Why don't I try to appease your mother? I could let her plan the wedding.'

'The one thing I do not intend to do is to change our plans to appease my mother.' The stubbornness was back in his voice. 'That's one of the reasons I love you. You have never buckled under to her.'

Blythe forced a smile, but made no response. She had her answers, but still she hesitated. Maybe Tate was right. Maybe it was the money. Was financial security so important to her that she was willing to marry a man she did not love and endure a perpetual battle with a mother-in-law who hated her? Still, she had got used to the idea of having someone to lean on and it was a difficult dream to give up.

'And speaking of Mother and gatherings,' George continued. 'She is planning one of her big parties next weekend and since you won't run away with me, I think we should use that opportunity to announce our engagement.'

'I doubt if your mother would be pleased to have one of her functions turned into an engagement party for us,' she played for more time.

'We won't tell her we plan to make the announcement. It can be a surprise. That way she won't have time to stew.' There was determination in his voice and she found herself agreeing to his plan while at the same time thinking that she should find a rock to crawl under.

'And the boys will have to attend,' he stipulated further. 'They've been so well-behaved lately I'm sure they will charm everyone and, just this once, I think you should dress them the same.'

The rest of the week passed in close to a fog for Blythe. She didn't want to face the truth. The thought of being alone again frightened her, yet she liked herself less and less with each passing day.

'You seem to have lost your fight,' Tate remarked one evening as he waited for the boys to finish a game of checkers. 'I sort of miss our little baiting sessions.'

'Well, I don't,' she replied honestly, keeping her attention focused on the sock she was darning.

'The boys tell me that you are planning to announce your engagement at a big party Mrs Lansky is giving this weekend.'

'George feels it is a good idea.' Still she continued to avoid looking up at him.

'I was under the impression that she and you didn't get along that well. I admit I was surprised to hear she was throwing this party for you and her son.'

Blythe ignored the challenge in his tone, answering almost absently, 'We don't, and she isn't. George simply thought that this party would be the perfect setting for the announcement, and plans to make it a surprise item on the agenda.'

'You're going to friction burn your finger,' Tate commented caustically, causing her to glance down and realise that she had stopped darning and was violently twisting her engagement ring. She stopped as he continued, 'I would like to watch this announcement. Is there any way I can get invited?'

'None,' she said firmly and, rising, went into her room followed by a piercing look from a pair of shuttered grey eyes.

After endless arguments with herself and still no firm decision reached, the time arrived to dress for the party. George had continued to be insistent about having the boys dress the same, and had bought them matching navy blue sports coats with white trousers, plus matching pairs of shoes.

They were not thrilled about this arrangement, but she convinced them that it could be looked upon as a game. They could see how many people could tell them apart. Once they were dressed, they tried the game on her first, but she had no trouble distinguishing one from the other. 'I'm your mother and mother's have a special talent for knowing their children,' she explained.

Next they tried it on Ethel. She guessed right the first time. However, when they denied she was correct, she was not certain enough to stand her ground and by the time they left, she was totally confused.

Blythe wondered why they had gone to see Ethel before Tate. The anxious looks on their faces gave her the answer. They were hesitant because it meant a great deal to them that the man be able to tell them apart. They did not want to face the possibility that he could not.

Blythe stood across the hall in her own doorway watching as he opened his door in answer to their knock. 'What's this?' he questioned with an amused smile. 'A pair of walking bookends?'

They didn't answer. They simply stood looking at him, practically holding their breaths.

'I see. I'm going to get the silent treatment until I've decided who is who. What happens if I'm wrong?'

Both little faces paled slightly, but still they remained silent.

'Okay, here goes.' Squatting down in front of them, he feigned a close scrutiny, looking behind their ears and at their teeth. Finally, scratching his head, he said, 'Eeny, meany, minny, moe I'm going to catch Roger by the toe.' Reaching down he wiggled one of the children's shoes.

'You're wrong.' The other child said while both kept their demeanour rigid.

'No, I'm not,' he returned firmly, and instantly both boys threw their arms around the man and hugged him.

'Tate can tell us apart,' Roger proudly informed his mother over his shoulder. 'Ethel couldn't, but Tate could.'

'I never doubted it for a minute,' she responded, then realised that she really hadn't. She had known as if it was a certainty that Tate would know each boy for himself. 'Come on, you two,' she called them back home. 'You have to comb your hair again before George arrives.'

Giving Tate a final hug, they ran past her laughing and plotting their ploys for the party.

'Isn't it a little dangerous to dress them alike?' Tate questioned, remaining in his doorway and addressing Blythe from across the hall.

'It was George's idea. He thought it would be cute.' There was a degree of tiredness in her voice.

'He might very soon live to regret his decision.' There was a chiding quality in his voice and she knew he was not only referring to George.

'You're right, Mr Calihan. He might. But as you pointed out, we all have to learn by our own mistakes.'

'Just keep in mind the cost of the mistake, Blythe. There are those that can be forgotten in a week, and there are those that you must live with for a lifetime.'

'You're becoming a regular philosopher, Mr Calihan,' she commented bitterly, not meeting his gaze as she stepped back and closed her door, placing the wooden barrier between herself and this self-appointed mentor.

Immediately upon his arrival, George realised his error. No matter how hard he tried, he couldn't keep the twins straight and they found this amusing. Finally putting an end to their antics, Blythe suggested that it was time to go and George happily agreed, but not before hinting that perhaps it would be better if they changed into more individualised outfits. This she refused to consider, explaining that she had a great deal of trouble convincing them to wear the same outfits and now that they were enjoying it, she didn't feel up to convincing them otherwise.

Mrs Lansky greeted the family group with some trepidation. 'This isn't a gathering for children.' Her displeasure was so strong it could not be totally hidden behind her polite façade.

Rewarding his mother with a look that squashed any further protests she might have considered, George said, 'I want our friends to meet Blythe and the boys. They will be members of our family very soon.'

Swallowing her rage, the woman excused herself to greet a newly arrived group of guests, leaving Blythe feeling like a gate-crasher.

It was a very large gathering and people were scattered throughout several rooms on the ground floor. 'The conservatory is probably the least crowded,' George suggested as he guided them in that direction.

It is also the room where the twins can do the least damage, Blythe added to herself. In fairness to George, she admitted that the paintings on the walls and the pieces of china and sculptures on the tables were expensive items and the boys did pose a threat to their safety. It wasn't that they were destructive. They merely possessed the natural curiosity of children. It was not difficult to visualise one of them dropping a delicate piece while taking a closer look, or bumping into a table and knocking one of the treasures to the floor. If they had been raised in this house they would know what to avoid, but as it was she had told them not to touch anything, which only made them want to examine everything.

At the door of the conservatory, he came to a sudden halt. 'I think the play-room would be a better idea.'

Glancing past him, Blythe saw Sherril Cooper sitting near the fountain talking to a grey-haired woman who left after a few moments. 'This room will be fine,' she said, passing him and walking purposefully towards Sherril, claiming the seat the older woman had vacated. 'It's so nice to see you again, Miss Cooper.'

'Please call me Sherril.' Although her demeanour was pleasant, the woman avoided looking at Blythe and, instead, concentrated on the twins. 'I thought you two never dressed alike,' she commented as they stood in front of her looking like duplicate prints of the same picture.

'George thought it would be fun this one time,' Brian explained.

'I didn't expect to see you here.' George's tone was close to accusatory as he looked down on the blonde-haired woman from his position behind the boys.

'My father was called away on a business emergency and I had to drive mother over.' Sherril's response sounded stilted as she met his gaze levelly.

Blythe could not deny the effect this man and woman had on one another. The tension became so thick it could have been cut with a knife. 'I would like a glass of wine,' she requested, breaking the icy silence following this explanation.

'Yes, of course.' George immediately left the room to fulfil her wishes.

The twins moved closer to the fountain to watch the fish, allowing the women to converse in private.

'Have you ever thought of fighting for him?' Blythe asked pointedly, deciding that the straightforward approach was best.

'Yes,' came the equally blunt response. 'And I think I might win if I was only fighting another woman. However, his mother's dislike of you and new-found admiration for me, has placed me at the disadvantage.'

'You do understand him,' Blythe mused.

'All men have their faults.'

'True.' A picture of Tate Calihan flashed into Blythe's mind. Erasing the disturbing image, she said, 'Tell me. How close did you and George come to getting married?'

'Almost to the altar. His mother fought us every step of the way, but we were so in love nothing she did could deter us. Then his father died and she suddenly had the advantage. His natural protective instinct surfaced. When he tried to explain to me that he had to call off the wedding because she needed him, I refused to understand. I threw his ring at him and left. I felt he had deserted me and he felt I had deserted him.'

'And you think I came along at a time when he was realising how much his mother had robbed him of and provided him with the perfect weapon for revenge?'

'Revenge is too harsh. Rebellion is more accurate.'

'Why didn't you come back sooner? You must have known you were playing a very dangerous game if you really wanted him back.'

'I didn't know what I wanted until I discovered the two

of you were engaged. I have a great deal of pride. That's why I didn't come back right away. I allowed myself to become so involved in my career I had no time to think, but now I realise that I have always cherished the day-dream that he would come searching for me.' Pausing, she frowned at Blythe. 'Are you attempting to size up the enemy in case I do decide to put up a fight?'

Before she could form an answer, George reappeared.

'Excuse me.' Sherril rose and moved towards the door. 'I have to find my mother.'

'What did you say to upset her?' he demanded of Blythe, watching the woman's retreating back.

'Nothing.'

'She would not get upset over nothing.'

'She's still in love with you.'

'And you don't know what you're talking about.' He downed the drink he was holding and stared at the fish in the pool.

A couple standing a few feet away looked towards them curiously.

'Whether I know what I am talking about or not, this is not the place to discuss this,' Blythe said, keeping her voice quiet. 'Would you mind making excuses for us to your mother and taking me and the boys home? I have a splitting headache.'

'Perhaps that would be for the best,' he agreed. 'This evening isn't exactly the happy occasion I had envisioned for announcing our engagement.'

While he went to find his mother, she gathered up the boys and led them towards the front door. When he joined them a few minutes later they were in their coats and ready to leave. The drive home was accomplished in a stoic silence that even the twins respected, remaining mute except for a few hushed whispers.

'You boys go play in your room. Your mother and I

have to talk,' George directed as soon as they had arrived at their destination and removed their coats.

'And close your door,' Blythe added. 'We want some privacy.'

The moment the latch clicked, George caught her by the shoulders and, staring hard into her face, asked, 'What made you say that Sherril is still in love with me?'

'She told me she is.'

Releasing her, he paced around the room. 'She left me when I needed her most. That's not an act of a woman in love.'

'She was very young and under the circumstances I can see how she might have been so hurt she felt she had to run away.' She knew she was possibly giving up her one chance for a secure future, but still she could not destroy another person's happiness for her own selfishness. Besides, if he really did love Sherril, the marriage would not last.

'She told you about our engagement and my father's death?' Anger was etched into every line of his face. This was not the George she knew.

'Enough. Not all of the details, but it was easy to fit the pieces together.'

'Why would she tell you?'

'I asked her.'

'You asked her?' He turned to face her, his expression incredulous.

'I'm not blind. I saw the way the two of you looked at one another. I knew there was something going on.'

'You're wrong, Blythe. I'm committed to you. You've carried the burden of raising the two boys for a long time and I promised you I would stay by your side, and I will.'

'I don't want a husband who is committed to me because of a principle. I want a husband who is committed to me because he loves me,' she explained in a calm voice. 'I'm giving you back your ring. You're a good man and I want you to be happy. You love Sherril as much as she loves you, or you wouldn't still be feeling the sting from the injury she caused you so long ago. I know the two of you can have a wonderful life together if you don't let your pride continue to stand between you. Keep in mind that a deeply abiding passionate love is not easy to find. Some people never discover it.'

For a long moment he stood staring down at the ring in his hand, then taking her hand gave it back. 'I want you to keep this as a gift. You're a remarkable woman and I'm proud to have known you. Someone else might have married me for my money and not worried about my happiness.'

'I really don't deserve . . .'

'Yes, you do.' He stopped her protest with a quick, friendly kiss, then left.

Dropping the ring on to a table, she sat down on the couch and stared into the empty room. Alone again—the words echoed through her mind. Kicking off her shoes, she curled her feet up under her and hugged herself tightly to stop the shaking. She had the boys and her job and maybe, some day, a man would come along who would satisfy her needs as well as those of the boys.

A sharp knock on the door startled her. She knew who it was and refused to respond. It sounded again, this time louder.

The twins' door opened and they came out slowly. 'Shall we answer the door?' Brian questioned, watching her worriedly.

'Yes, go ahead. He'll probably take it off of its hinges if you don't.' She felt more weary than she had ever felt in her life.

'Blythe, open up!' Tate's voice sounded from the other side of the barrier.

Roger had the door open almost immediately.

'What's going on!?' Tate strode into the room assuring himself that the boys were all right before spotting Blythe curled up on the couch.

'You were right,' Roger was saying as he followed Tate towards his mother. 'She isn't going to marry George.'

'What's he talking about?' Blythe glared up at the man standing in front of her. When he didn't answer, she turned towards Brian. 'What is Roger talking about?'

'Tate promised us that if we were good, you wouldn't marry George.' The words came out hesitantly as the child looked from one adult to the other.

'Wasn't that clever of him,' she commented drily.

'Not clever enough.' Tate broke his silence. 'I notice you still have the ring.' With a nod of his head, he indicated the jewel lying on the table.

'George gave it to me as a gift because I'm such a wonderful person.' She met his gaze, daring him to contradict George's assessment.

'Mom,' Roger crawled up next to her, pulling her attention away from the man towering over her. 'Our father was the one deeply . . .' he paused, searching for the word.

'Abiding,' Brian filled the gap.

'Deeply abiding passionate love of your life, wasn't he?' the child finished gazing up into her face, his eyes wide with expectation.

'What?' His question had caught her by surprise.

'We overheard you tell George that a person is really lucky if they find a deeply abiding passionate love once in their life,' Brian elaborated, crawling up next to her on the side opposite his brother.

'And you're so special we know our father must have loved you that way,' Roger picked up the thread, 'and you must have loved him that way and he would have loved us. Wouldn't he have?'

'Yes, of course, he would have loved you.' Slow hot tears began to roll down her cheeks as she wrapped an arm around each child.

Roger, in one of his curious moments of adult comprehension, looked up at the big man standing before them and, with a deadly serious expression, said, 'Maybe you should leave. I think Mom wants to be alone with us for a while.'

Black thunder rolled over the man's features before the shuttered look returned and, nodding acceptance of the request, he left.

# CHAPTER SIX

DRAGGING herself out of bed the next morning, Blythe fixed the usual Sunday morning pancakes. Although no formal arrangements had been made, she set a place for Tate at the boys' insistence, reminding herself that the man had never been shy about entering into their private life. When he had not put in an appearance by the time the twins had finished eating, Roger became anxious.

'Maybe he's mad at me 'cause I asked him to leave last night.'

'I'm sure he understood,' she assured the child.

'Maybe he over slept like you did last Sunday,' he persisted.

'Or maybe he simply decided to skip church and sleep in this morning,' she countered.

'Or maybe he's sick and needs help,' Brian interjected.

Brian's suggestion disturbed Blythe. As angry as Tate made her, she would not like to see him in need of help with no one there to offer aid. Instructing the boys to get dressed, she started across the hall, only to stop almost immediately as her eye was caught by the note taped to her door.

'Is it from Tate?' Roger demanded, miss-buttoning his shirt while giving her his full attention.

'I thought you were supposed to be in your room dressing,' she frowned, not wanting to read the message in front of the child in case it was a farewell note. If the man was gone for good she wanted to prepare the boys before telling them.

'I wanted to be sure Tate was all right.' He looked up at her defensively.

Brian, still in the process of fastening his trousers, joined them. 'Is Tate sick?'

'No.' Tearing open the envelope, she glanced quickly at the note, then with a feeling of relief read the message to the boys. It was short and to the point, saying only that a problem had come up on his ranch that he had to see to personally. He promised to be back soon.

The boys instantly had all kinds of ideas about what he meant by trouble and spent all day discussing several very romantic improbabilities.

Roger's favourite was cattle rustlers. 'Do you think Tate might get shot or even killed chasing them?' he asked his mother when she tucked him into bed that night.

'No bad guy could ever hurt Tate,' Brian had proclaimed firmly.

'And I doubt that there are very many cattle rustlers left,' Blythe added.

'You're wrong, Mom,' Brian informed her. 'I saw it on television. They use trucks instead of riding horses, but they do carry guns and are dangerous.'

'I'm sure Tate can take care of himself,' she reaffirmed, throwing Brian a cautionary look.

'Sure he can,' Brian agreed, and Roger smiled, having been convinced.

That night as she slept, Blythe dreamt of cowboys on horseback and wild herds thundering across rugged terrain. They were scenes and events recalled from hundreds of western movies she had watched as a kid. Suddenly, Tate was riding at the front of a band of men and shots were being fired. He fell from his horse, and Blythe woke up crying, her heart pounding against her chest. Drying her eyes, she sat up in bed, and in the stillness of the night tried to calm her shaken nerves. The past couple of weeks played through her mind and she suddenly saw Tate as a catalyst in all that had happened. George's proposal had followed Tate's entrance. Admittedly George had talked about getting married for a long time, but she had sometimes questioned whether their relationship would actually reach that stage. It had been Tate's presence that had nudged the man into action.

Then there was Tate's harassment of her. If he had not made her question her motives and feelings more closely, she would have kept them buried and married George. Considering what she now knew, it would have been a disastrous arrangement.

Lying back down, she closed her eyes only to find Tate's image filling her mind. It was so very vivid, from the thick black hair to the mocking grey eyes and the hard square jaw. There was something about the face. Those grey eyes. A wild spasm of fear shook her. Tate Calihan had the same strange, grey-coloured eyes that her sons had. Breathing deeply she tried to reason her fear away. Why would anyone come looking for them after seven years? If the father had been interested in them surely he would have sought them out sooner. The matching eye colour had to be a simple coincidence. Besides, why would he play this cat-and-mouse game? Convincing herself that she was over-reacting because of the tension she had been under the past couple of weeks, she tried to get some sleep before Monday morning.

The bank was buzzing the next morning with the news that George Lansky had eloped over the weekend. 'I never thought of him as being romantic enough or as passionate enough to do such a thing,' Mildred remarked as she arranged her money for the day.

'I suppose it was a matter of finding the right woman,' Blythe suggested quietly.

'Don't tell me you are one of those romantics who thinks

that there is only one right man for each woman,' Hazel chided.

'I didn't say that,' Blythe defended herself.

'Don't let Hazel bother you,' Sally interjected. 'She really believes in the "one right man" theory. That's why she's been married and divorced three times. She's still looking for him.'

As the bantering continued, Blythe breathed a grateful sigh that she and George had not made their relationship public.

At the same time that Blythe was breathing her sigh of relief, Tate Calihan was eating breakfast at his ranch. Ruth Fleetdeer poured his second cup of coffee with a worried expression on her normally cheerful face. She had been the housekeeper for the Calihans since Tate's and Mike's mother had died and did not like what was happening to this oldest son. When he had been younger, before their father's death, he had charmed the ladies with his smile, and had always been quick with a laugh and an encouraging word. But now it was as if a black cloud hung over him.

'Did you find what you were looking for in St Louis?' she asked.

'More than I bargained for,' he frowned. His lips pressed tightly together indicated that he wished to say no more. Respecting his silence, she left, knowing that he would tell her what she needed to know when the time came.

Later that morning, after a long snow-inhibited drive, Tate walked down the corridor of the hospital which had been his true destination when he had left St Louis. His expression was grim as he entered a private room where the shell of what had once been a healthy man lay in the bed, tubes running into and out of the emaciated body.

'Mr Calihan,' the private nurse greeted him in the hushed whisper that came so naturally after all her years in this restrained environment. 'Your brother has just gone back to sleep, but I do hope you have time to wait for him to awaken. He asks for you constantly.'

'And he's asking for him now,' a harsh, slightly sleep-drugged voice said from the bed.

'Now I could have sworn you were asleep.' The white-clad woman approached her patient and began to take his pulse.

'It's still beating, or I wouldn't be talking to you. I'd be down in Hell where my brother thinks I belong. Now, get out of here and let us talk.' The man attempted to pull free of her hold.

Only the slightest flicker in the nurse's eyes showed that she had heard his words as she finished taking his pulse. Over the years, she had been subjected to a great deal of abuse from the sick and dying. It was a circumstance of her occupation and she accepted it as such.

'I apologise for my brother,' Tate addressed her in a controlled tone. 'However, we do need to discuss a family matter that requires privacy. Why don't you take a break. Have some coffee in the cafeteria.'

Although the request was politely issued, the woman knew it was an order. 'Have the floor nurse page me when you are finished,' she instructed, then left.

'You find her, Tate?' Mike Calihan demanded harshly, as the door swung closed.

'I found her.' Tate's mouth was a hard line and his stance rigid.

'You sure took your time.'

'She was planning to marry. I had to wait around to make sure it didn't happen.'

'Were you playing protector for her or the man?' A harsh laugh followed this question. When Tate did not answer, the dying man said, 'Is she as pretty as I remember? All that auburn hair that looks like tarnished copper in the sunlight and auburn eyes that spark with fire when she's angry.'

'Yes.' Tate's voice was liquid ice.

'Even as I lie here on my death bed, you hate me, don't you?' There was a whimper in the man's voice.

'You ruined your life and took a better man's to boot.'

'And you had me locked up like an animal!' The words exploded in a vengeful shriek.

'You had become an animal,' Tate responded levelly. 'You were a danger to yourself and to everyone around you.'

'It was the drugs.' Again the whimper was back. 'You're so self-righteous.' A throaty, bitter chuckle issued from the bed. 'Did she tell you what she did with the kid? My bet is that she didn't.'

'The kid turned out to be twin boys, and she has them with her.'

'That can't be. She told me she was going to get rid of whatever was born. Are you sure you found the right woman and that the kids are Calihans?' This news had agitated the dying man.

'They have the Calihan eyes, though I have to admit it puzzles me that the woman doesn't seem to know our name.' There was an expectant, almost hopeful look in the dark man's eyes.

'She wouldn't. I was using the name Mike Masters at the time. Didn't want to besmirch the Calihan brand.'

The shuttered look returned to the visitor's eyes.

'I admit this does lighten my revenge on you, Tate,' Mike continued in a musing vein. 'I had hoped you would never find the little bastard,' here he paused to correct himself, 'bastards. I was counting on it always gnawing at you that there were Calihans out there somewhere and you couldn't get your hands on them.'

Tate stood silently staring down on this shell of a human being who had once been the kid brother he had loved.

'I was the first man to ever have her. That's something special.' A light flashed in Mike's eyes. 'Maybe that was why she kept them. I sure would like to see her again.'

'I had something like that in mind.'

'Now why would you want to perform such a good deed for your brother?'

'I think it's time you legitimised the boys.'

'You mean like in the Bible where I pass my hand over them and claim them as mine in front of God and all others?' There was ridicule in Mike's voice.

'I mean that you and their mother should exchange marriage vows.' There was an uneasy bitterness in the words as Tate spoke.

Mike laughed. 'You've got to be kidding.' More laughter. 'You want me to perform a death-bed repentance. A final gesture in an effort to wash away the sins of a lifetime.'

'They deserve to have the Calihan name.'

'You bring her here to me and I'll think about it real serious,' the man in the bed bargained.

Tate rose without responding and moved towards the door.

'I want to see her. You can't deny a dying man his final wish.'

'In your case, I could,' Tate threw back. 'But like you said, I'll think about it.'

A chuckle rose from the bed. 'You'll bring her. You can't stand the thought of those two boys without their marvellous natural heritage of the Calihan name.'

That night Tate reread the report Harvey Adams had

provided him. The details concerning Blythe Walters' past were very sketchy. The man had been instructed to find the woman and gather as much information about her present circumstances as was possible without making her suspicious. Tate hadn't wanted her to bolt before they caught up with her.

The page containing the information concerning the accident in which the aunt and sister had died held his attention. His jaw twitched as his expression hardened into black marble. The sister's body had been so badly mangled that the coroner had insisted on medical records to verify the identity of the victim. There was no doubt that the woman who had died was Brenda Walters.

# CHAPTER SEVEN

'TATE'S not back yet.' Roger greeted his mother with the same pronouncement he had greeted her with for the past five days, and each day his face had looked a little sadder and his voice had sounded less hopeful.

Blythe tried to cheer him up, but she, too, was suffering from an attack of depression. In all honesty she did not regret George's departure. However, for some reason, the sense of aloneness she had learned so long ago to live with was stronger than it had ever been before.

Brian had remained stoically reserved through the week, glancing up at Tate's note stuck in the letter-box several times a day and nodding with that look that said he knew the man would be returning soon.

'Roger, please eat your dinner,' Blythe was pleading as she watched her son push his food around on his plate, but not carry any to his mouth, when a knock sounded on the door. Both boys flew out of their chairs and before she could utter a word had the door open and had thrown themselves into Tate's waiting arms. 'It's a good thing it was you,' she said as the man entered carrying one boy under each arm, 'and not some unsuspecting stranger.'

'We'd know Tate's knock anywhere,' Roger chided his mother.

'I don't know how. He so seldom uses it.' She tried to keep her tone indifferent, but inside she found herself wanting to laugh and cry, both at the same time. For some unfathomable reason she had missed this arrogant Wyomian as much as the boys and she would have sold her soul at that moment to be in those strong arms.

'Same old Blythe,' he noted drily, lowering the boys.

'You're just in time for dinner,' Brian announced, taking Tate's hand and leading the man towards the table.

'Now, wait a minute. I didn't mean to impose. I only stopped by to let you know I was back.'

'There's plenty,' Blythe heard herself offering. He looked tired, as if he hadn't slept well in days.

'You sure?'

'Sure, she's sure,' Roger grabbed Tate's other hand, joining his brother's effort.

'Okay, okay,' he laughed. It was a warm, loving sound and Blythe wished she was a part of it, but instinctively knew she was excluded.

During the meal, Roger bombarded Tate with questions about cattle rustlers.

'He thinks that is why you were gone,' she explained.

'It was rustlers, wasn't it?' The child gazed up into the man's face, the pain he had suffered by Tate's sudden departure evident in his eyes. 'I know it had to be something as important as that for you to leave like you did.'

'It wasn't rustlers, but it was something important,' the man assured him. Then, before they could probe further, he guided the conversation back to the boys' world, asking them what they had been doing in school and during the evenings.

Blythe caught herself studying the man closely for any strong resemblance to the boys. It was difficult to differentiate between actual similarities and imagined ones. After a while she gave up, convincing herself that the eye colour was merely a coincidence and she was making a mountain out of a mole hill.

After dinner the twins insisted that Tate play them each a game of checkers. When Blythe suggested that he might be too tired after his long trip, he rewarded her show of concern with a cynically raised eyebrow as if to say he saw through her ploy to get rid of him. Stifling a yawn he acquiesced to the boys' request.

Again feeling shut out, she turned her attention to the dinner dishes while Brian and Roger played each other a warm-up game as a way of deciding who would play Tate first. Determined to win, Roger deliberated over his moves and, by the time they completed this mildly prolonged game, they discovered that their third player had fallen asleep in his chair. Tiptoeing around, they tried not to wake him.

When Blythe joined them, they tried to convince her to allow Tate to stay. 'He'll wake up all crooked and sore if you leave him in that chair all night,' she explained and they both agreed that they did not want that to happen. Shaking the man gently, she said, 'Tate. Wake up. You have to go home.'

The man's eyes opened slowly. 'Sorry guys. Guess your mom was right. I am really bushed.'

'I'll help you over to your place,' Blythe said with a resigned sigh, knowing from his blurry-eyed look that he still wasn't completely awake. 'Where is your key?'

'In my trouser pocket,' he yawned.

Reaching into his pocket, the feel of the man's lean muscles so close to her skin caused a disturbingly unsettling sensation to sweep over her. Grabbing the key, she extracted her hand rapidly. 'Come on. I have it.'

As they crossed the hall, she allowed him to lean on her in his semi-conscious state. Following her instructions, the boys protestingly remained at home. Walking him into the bedroom, she eased him on to the bed and then unfastened a couple of the buttons of his shirt. To her dismay, tears began to flood her eyes. Only her pride kept them from spilling over. How could she care about a man who disliked her so strongly? Admitting to herself for the first time how intensely she had felt his sudden departure, she realised that for her it had been like a slap in the face. It was as if he had deliberately left the moment her engagement was broken as a blunt way of letting her know that he wasn't available to take George's place.

Wanting to escape from the room, she moved quickly to his boots. Getting the heavy leather footwear off was a struggle, and she couldn't help thinking that maybe that was why cowboys always talked about dying with their boots on. Dropping the second one on the floor next to the first, she started towards the door.

'Blythe,' Tate spoke her name in a groggy voice.

'What do you want?' she questioned, moving back towards the bed.

In response, his lean sinewy hand came up to catch her arm and, before she knew what was happening, he had pulled her down over him and on to the bed. Rolling over, he pinned her down with the long length of his body. 'I never greeted you properly.' His words were a low whisper as his lips descended on hers, awakening fires he seemed so easily to spark. She had no will to struggle against him, greeting his kiss like a thirsty man being offered water. It was as if his arms were the safe harbour she had sought all these years and she wanted to remain there for ever.

'You taste good,' he murmured, his warm breath stirring the hair near her ear before his mouth began its sensual exploration of her neck.

Smiling happily, she snuggled closer to him, drinking in the feel of him while his hands moved caressingly over the soft curves of her body and his lips once again sampled her mouth.

'Mom, is everything okay?' Roger's anxious voice sounded from Tate's living-room.

Suddenly embarrassed, not wanting the twins to find

her in such a compromising position, she rolled out of the man's relaxed grasp and off the bed. Tate muttered a regretful moan, but made no attempt to recapture her.

'Everything is fine,' she called back, lifting the bedspread and throwing it over the prone figure on the bed who was now once again fully asleep.

'Can we help?' Brian asked as two little heads peeped into the room.

'No, I think he'll be all right like that for the night,' she replied. Then feeling the need to explain her long absence, added, 'It took me for ever to get his boots off.'

The boys nodded as if they understood fully, and all three tiptoed out of the room.

Later, as Blythe lay in her bed, the remembered sensation of Tate's lips caused a warmth to spread over her and a soft smile to light up her face. She must have misread him, because his actions on the bed had not been ones of dislike. Perhaps her future was not as black as she had envisioned. Drifting into a peaceful sleep, her sense of loneliness vanished.

The next morning, as was typical of Saturday mornings, she cleaned while her sons watched television. They had wanted to call Tate and invite him over as soon as they were up and although she, too, wanted to see the man as badly as the boys, she refused to allow it. He had looked so tired the night before, she didn't want to take a chance on disturbing his rest. They settled for waiting until eleven and then asking him over for lunch.

However, they did not have to wait that long. His familiar knock sounded on the door around ten o'clock and as the boys rushed to let him in, Blythe found herself holding her breath. Her heart sank to her feet as he turned towards her, the shuttered look back in his eyes. The glow from the kiss vanished and her sense of loneliness returned.

The twins attempted to claim his attention, but he put them off, explaining that he had an important matter to discuss with their mother.

'You going to ask her to marry you and take us back to your ranch?' Roger looked up at him expectantly.

'Not exactly.' There was a guardedness even as he spoke to the child which surprised Blythe.

Roger looked towards his brother questioningly. Brian shrugged his shoulder, but remained silent. They both sensed a tenseness about the man they did not understand.

Assuming that he wanted to discuss how he was going to ease his way out of the twins' lives, Blythe schooled her face not to show her disappointment. In a voice she hoped sounded coolly indifferent, she said, 'I suppose we should talk at your place.'

'Yes, that would be best. And, boys, we want some privacy,' he cautioned, letting them know that interruptions would not be looked upon kindly.

Entering his living-room, she said, 'I assume you will be going back to Wyoming to stay very soon.'

'Yes.' With a sweep of his hand, he indicated that he would like her to sit on the couch while he chose a chair opposite her position. 'First, I want to apologise for any out of line behaviour I might have shown last night. I have a very vague recollection of kissing someone female and, although I was dreaming about a girl I know back home, I believe I may have substituted you.'

'You said my name.' Hurtful confusion filled her eyes. Why was he doing this? Why hadn't he simply not mentioned the episode in his bedroom, pretended he never realised it had happened. Why did he feel he had to wound her by making her feel like a cheap substitute. 'Do you know another Blythe?'

'I've known a lot of women,' he returned drily.

Swallowing her pain, a wall of ice formed around her heart and she met his gaze with cold, reserved silence.

'I believe we have some family business to discuss.'

'Yes,' she agreed. 'We have to decide how you are going to work yourself out of my sons' lives.'

'No. What we have to discuss is how we are going to legitimise them,' he corrected.

'I don't understand.' Fear made speaking difficult.

'Let me begin a different way. The long-lost, deeply abiding, passionate love of your life wants to see you.' Tate's manner was black.

The colour drained from her face. 'What . . . what are you talking about? Who are you?'

'I'm the twins' uncle. I admit I was confused when you didn't know my name, but my brother explained to me that he was using the name Masters when you two knew each other.'

'No.' The word came out in a moan as she slumped backwards in a faint.

'Blythe, dammit, wake up.' Though the words were harshly delivered, there was concern in Tate's tone.

Her eyes fluttered open, then closed again to shut out the anxiousness she had read in his expression. He was swabbing her face with a damp cloth, and reaching up she pushed his hand away. He could not fool her this time. She hardened herself against him, determined that he would not destroy her world.

Leaving the cloth on her forehead, he moved back to his chair. Slowly she reopened her eyes and, taking the cloth in her hand, swung her legs off the couch and herself into a sitting position. Breathing deeply, she tried to overcome the dizziness in her head and stop the nausea in her stomach. After a minute or two she started to rise, hoping her need to escape was great enough to keep her legs from collapsing.

'Sit.' Tate's tone was uncompromising. 'You don't want to have this out in front of the boys, do you?'

Looking up, she met the silvered steel of his eyes and was glad she had not fallen for his act of concern. Sinking back on to the couch, she fought to clear the panic from her mind. With a conviction as solid as granite she met his gaze once again. 'I don't care who you are. You have no right to interfere in my life or in my sons' lives.'

'Their natural father is interested in the family he abandoned. He would like to see them. He would like to make amends.'

'He will not see me or my, and I emphasise the word "my", children. I do not want anything from him.'

'The boys are Calihans. They have a right to their family name.'

'As far as I'm concerned, that's a right they are better off overlooking.' It was a shot meant to wound and from the darkening of Tate's eyes she knew she had found her mark.

'What about that sad tale you threw at me about being all alone in this world. Wouldn't you like to know that the boys have a real family who can care for them if anything should happen to you?' He was using her own words against her.

'Considering the family, the answer is no.'

Tate drew a sharp, angry breath. 'You know nothing about the Calihans.'

'I know enough. You have a brother who abandoned a young girl after he got her pregnant, and your actions don't speak very well either. You come sneaking into our lives, looking us over before disclosing your true identity. Why? Did you want to make sure the boys were good enough for your precious family heritage before you broke the news?'

'No. From the moment I saw them I knew I would be

proud to be their uncle.' His eyes softened momentarily when he spoke of the boys, then hardened again as he continued, 'I didn't want you running off to marry good old George in order to escape your responsibility to provide the boys with their rightful parentage.'

'You . . . you stayed around, butting into our lives, just to make certain that I didn't marry George?' she stammered as the truth dawned on her.

'Precisely. The boys are Calihans.'

'What if I had been in love with him? You had no right!'

'Either you weren't in love with George, or any man would do for you, considering your reaction to me,' he noted sardonically.

'You're a lot of things that aren't in my vocabulary, but I'm sure they are in yours, Tate Calihan, so pick a few,' she spat back at him, her eyes red with fury.

'And,' he continued, undaunted by her tirade, 'I have every right to interfere in your life as long as you are the mother of a Calihan.'

'You never thought that was so important before. It's been seven years.'

'I didn't know of your existence until a few months ago when my brother saw fit to provide me with a few sordid details of his past.'

The inflection he placed on the word 'sordid' brought an angry flush to Blythe's cheeks. 'How far would you have gone to prevent my marriage,' she asked in a low, controlled voice, needing to know her enemy's boundaries. There was no doubt in her mind that Tate was her enemy.

'I would have told him the truth. That the boys' father was alive and that you were involved with drugs and alcohol and running with a wild crowd when they were conceived.'

'You're talking about a child of sixteen. Are you so perfect you've never made a mistake?'

'I've made plenty, but we're not talking about me and we're not really talking about you. We're talking about the future of those two boys in your living-room.'

'You can't talk about their future without talking about me. They're my sons, Tate Calihan. They're all I have and you're not taking them away from me. Not ever!' Her fingernails dug into the palms of her hands as her fists tightened.

'I wasn't suggesting taking them away from you.' His tone was coldly patronising. 'I merely want to see the boys legitimised. To put it bluntly, you and their father are going to do what you should have done seven years ago. You are going to wed one another.'

'You're crazy. You can't go around ordering other people to do what you think is right. You don't know everything.' The inside of Blythe's mouth felt like cotton as she fought to keep her voice steady. 'I have no intention of ever seeing your brother, much less marrying him. He's never going to touch me.'

'Touch you again,' he corrected.

'Touch me again,' the words came out in a choked whisper.

'Considering your attitude, I guess it's lucky for the both of you that he is incapable of making the attempt,' Tate noted in a sarcastically musing tone.

'What do you mean by that?'

'The man is dying. It will be a death-bed union. Then you will legitimately be the widow you claim to be.'

'You're certain he is dying?' She didn't trust this man.

'He has advanced cancer.'

'He could have a remission,' she challenged, fighting for time to think. There had to be a way out of this.

'He is past that stage.'

'If I agreed to go along with this farce, do I have your word you will leave me and the boys alone afterwards?' she bargained, knowing even as she said the words it was a futile hope. Tate's attachment to her sons was too genuine.

'The boys are Calihans. They should know their family. As my sister-in-law, no one can object to your living on the ranch with me. I'll take care of you and the boys and they will grow up knowing the land their pioneer forefathers died for.'

'No. The boys and I will remain living here in St Louis and they may visit you once in a while.'

'No good, Blythe. But all of this is in the future, anyway. We'll discuss it at a later date. Right now we have a more immediate concern. We need to tell the boys who I am, and you need to pack. We all leave for Wyoming tonight.'

'That's impossible. I can't just take a leave of absence from my job like that with no advance notice. What would I tell my boss? Surely you don't expect me to tell him I need a few days off to go marry a man on his death-bed so my sons will have their father's name.'

'I don't care what you tell him, but you are coming with me today. If necessary, I will go to Mrs Lansky and explain the situation to her personally. After that, I don't think you will need to worry about your job.'

Blythe swallowed hard. 'All right. I'll make the necessary arrangements. But the boys shouldn't miss school. They can stay here with Ethel.'

'No, Blythe. They are coming, too.' Tate's tone was uncompromising.

'And what are you going to tell them? They think their father is dead and that he had no family.' Her stomach was churning wildly.

'They have to know the truth sooner or later.'

'No!' The word came out in a scream of panic. 'You can't do that to them or to me. If you hurt us like that, I promise you, I'll see that you regret it for the rest of your life.'

'I guessed that you would not be willing to deal with the truth,' his voice dripped with cynicism. 'Therefore, I have come up with a plausible lie. We will tell them that years ago their father and I had an argument and he left home vowing never to return. I never knew what had happened to him until a few months ago when an army buddy of his stopped by the ranch looking for work. The man told me that my brother was dead, but that he had left a pregnant wife behind. I immediately hired a detective to find this mother and child for me.'

'I suppose I have no choice?' She choked back the tears, determined not to give this man the satisfaction of seeing her cry.

'None. Now shall we go talk to the boys.' It was a command rather than a question. 'The plane leaves in four hours.'

Squaring her shoulders, Blythe rose and walked towards the door like a prisoner on her way to a firing squad. 'Is your father willing to go along with the lie? And what about the rest of your family?'

'My father is dead and there is no close family living in Wyoming. When the time comes, we'll tell them what is necessary.' Tate's hand closed around her arm. 'Keep in mind that this is a joyful occasion. You have just discovered that your beloved husband had a brother who wants to be close to you and your sons.'

'Let go of me!' she cried, attempting to pull free from his grasp.

Tightening his hold, he pulled her up against his long muscular frame. 'Be careful. I can be a very dangerous enemy.'

'Especially towards women and small boys,' she retorted, flicking her head in a gesture of disgust.

With his free hand, he caught her chin and turned her face upward. Grey thunder met red fury. 'How could you lower yourself to my brother's level?' There was intense bitterness in his words.

'At the moment, I don't see much difference between his level and yours.'

For a moment she thought he was going to strike her. Physically adjusting to accept the blow, she suddenly felt herself being released. In response to the nod of his head, she opened the door and walked across the hall, prudently refraining from further comments.

'You look a little sick, Mom,' Brian noted as his mother and Tate entered. 'Did Tate smoke one of his long brown cigarettes in front of you?'

'No.' Blythe coughed to clear her throat. 'I've just had a little shock and need some time to get over it.'

Both boys watched with interest as Tate's arm circled their mother's shoulders.

Feeling the warning pressure of his touch, she forced a smile. 'It seems that your father did have a family after all.'

Sensing her hesitation, Tate took over. 'I hope you boys will be as happy about this as I am. Your father was my brother, so that makes you my nephews, and me your uncle.'

'Our uncle?' The twins stared at the man incredulously.

Feeling the need to soften the blow now that it had been delivered, Blythe moved away from Tate and joined the boys on the couch. 'Your father and Tate had an argument when they were younger. It was like the ones you two have only much much worse, and they stopped speaking to each other. Your father went so far as to leave his home. That was when I met him. He never wrote Tate about me. However, a few months ago, a man who had known your father in the army came by the ranch looking for work and told Tate about our existence. He then started looking for us.'

'Why didn't you tell us right away who you were?' Roger demanded, eyeing Tate sceptically with the hurtful look of a child who has discovered his hero has a flaw.

'He wanted to give us a chance to get to know him as a friend before we had to accept him as a relative.' Blythe found herself making excuses to spare her son's feelings.

'Maybe he wasn't sure if he wanted us,' Roger suggested blackly, not willing to accept his mother's explanation blindly.

'That's not true.' Tate knelt in front of the boy. 'From the first moment I saw you, I knew I would be proud to have you for my nephew. Both of you,' he looked towards Brian, including him. There was an open, honest quality in the man's voice and a gentleness in his gaze. 'I only hope that the two of you will be happy to have me as your uncle.'

Both boys looked towards their mother for her confirmation, and she knew she could destroy Tate in their eyes for ever at this moment, but she couldn't bring herself to do that. As much as he hated her, he loved the boys and they needed him. With a tearful, affirmative nod she released them.

'Women always cry when they are happy,' Brian offered in a philosophical manner, explaining his mother's tears both to himself and to the man he now knew as his uncle. Then, sliding off the couch, he extended his hand for a masculine handshake.

Remaining in a kneeling position to allow full eye contact, Tate accepted the small hand. Roger joined them. When the handshakes had been completed, the twins continued to stand in front of the man, their legs spread slightly apart and their hands clasped behind their backs. It suddenly dawned on Blythe how very like miniature Tate's they were. What they lacked in looks, they made up for in manner. Uncle Tate might have bitten off more than he could chew, she thought acidly to herself.

Facing the Wyomian squarely, Brian spoke. 'We know that our father was not married to our mother.'

Blythe bit her lip, but said nothing. She had suspected that they had guessed the truth. However, they had never chosen to bring their questions to her and she had not pressed them, feeling that when they felt the time was right they would come to her.

'That's why our name is Walters and not Calihan,' Roger added. 'But we don't mind because we have the greatest mom in the world.'

'And we know that he would have married her if he hadn't had to go away to war so fast,' Brian finished.

'You're right,' Tate agreed, meeting their gazes with sincerity. 'Any man would be proud to have your mother for his wife and you for his children.'

Blythe's hand went up to her mouth to stifle the cry of pain that threatened to escape. If only he had meant the first half of that statement. The thought reverberated in her mind as she unwillingly admitted that if he had loved her, she could have returned that love completely. However, he hated her, and she returned that hate instead.

'And to prove to you how strongly I feel,' Tate continued, not once looking up at Blythe, 'I'm going to take you to see my ranch.'

'When?' the twins questioned in the same breath.

'Today.'

'Today? Can we go to Wyoming and get back by Monday?' Roger's eyes were wide with surprise.

'That wouldn't give you much time to see my ranch. You're going to have to miss a little bit of school,' Tate apologised.

'We won't mind missing school, but mom might not like it,' Brian looked towards Blythe.

'And Mom has to be back for work,' Roger interjected. 'You do want her to come, too, don't you?'

'I wouldn't think of going back without your mother,' Tate assured them, and this time his eyes met hers with a warning.

'This is a special occasion,' she said, forcing a smile. 'You boys go pick out a couple of toys to bring along while I pack and make a few phone calls.' Rising swiftly, she escaped into her room. Closing the door, she stood against the hard wooden structure for support until her legs stopped shaking. There had to be a way out of this mess, but she didn't have the presence of mind to think of it at the moment.

The next couple of hours were frantic. She told Ethel just enough of the truth to pacify the woman, while telling the bank manager a total lie. The packing was chaotic even with Tate's guidance. He helped the boys select their warmest clothing and warned Blythe to expect bitter winter weather.

'Will we meet the Indian lady who works for you when we get to your ranch?' Brian questioned on the way to the airport in the taxi.

'She'll probably have dinner ready for us,' Tate confirmed.

The thought of food turned Blythe's stomach. Tate had made the boys sandwiches while she finished the packing, but when he had brought one to her she had excused herself and gone into the bathroom and been sick.

'What time will we be getting to Wyoming?' Brian

asked as he tried to keep pace with Tate through the terminal.

'Almost the same time we leave here.'

'But I thought it was a long ways away.' The child looked confused.

'It is, but we pick up two hours during the flight,' Tate said. Then, leaving them, he went to complete the arrangements for their trip.

Brian looked towards his mother.

'He means,' she explained, 'that in Wyoming right now it is two hours earlier than it is here.'

'Why?'

'It has something to do with time zones,' she replied with a shrug, then indicating the large-windowed wall facing the landing strips, said, 'Why don't you two go watch the planes.'

This was the first time the boys had flown and they needed no further encouragement. She was standing several feet behind them when Tate rejoined her. 'You didn't eat any lunch,' he said stiffly. 'Can I get you something from the coffee shop?'

She shook her head and continued to watch the boys.

'This isn't the end of the world.' His voice was harsh with exasperation. 'Try to think of it as a new beginning.'

'Please.' She looked up at him, her eyes a soft pleading brown behind the thick glistening shield of unshed tears. 'Please, let me take the boys home and give me some time to get used to all of this. I promise I won't run away.'

'There is no time. Mike is dying.'

'You can't really want me to marry a dying man?' Looking hard into his eyes, she tried to read behind the shuttered mask he wore, but it was no use and she turned away.

The boarding call for their flight sounded over the speaker system and, with a sigh, she followed Tate as he collected the twins and they walked towards the proper area. Once on board, each twin wanted a seat by the window. To make this arrangement possible, Blythe found herself seated next to Tate. Too emotionally exhausted to care, she drifted into the sleep of escape almost as soon as the plane was in the air.

'Blythe, wake up. We're almost ready to land,' Tate's voice quietly coaxed her back to awareness.

Refusing to heed his words, she moved her cheek in a gentle caressing manner against the sturdy arm that had supported her during most of the flight. The warmth of his skin through the fabric of the shirt gave a feeling of security. Security! Suddenly reality impinged upon her, and Blythe sat upright. She had been leaning against Tate, and he could never be considered a source of security for her.

'Are you feeling better?' he questioned.

'Better than what?' she muttered.

'Obviously not.' He frowned.

'Obviously not what?' Brian asked coming to stand in the aisle next to Tate's chair. Roger joined him.

'Have you two boys been running up and down the aisle while I was asleep?' she demanded, ignoring the child's question.

'They've been perfect gentlemen, Mrs Calihan,' a passing stewardess paused to assure her. 'You have a lovely family.' Then with a quick smile which encompassed all of them, she moved on to her other passengers.

Blythe shot Tate a covertly hostile glance while Roger and Brian beamed at one other.

'She knows we belong together,' Brian whispered to his mother happily, then walking arm in arm, he and his brother made their hundredth trip to the magazine rack.

'I made the reservations in my name. Considering the strong family resemblance, the woman's mistake was natural and I didn't think you would want me to take the time to explain our situation to a stranger.'

She ignored the hint of a challenge in his voice. He could bait her all he wanted, but she wasn't playing. Outwardly, she continued to maintain a calm disposition, although inwardly she felt as if she was going to collapse. There had to be a way of avoiding the man in the hospital.

On disembarking from the plane in Casper, Wyoming, they were met by a short plump man in his early fifties wearing a big stetson, faded jeans, western boots and a heavy sheepskin coat.

'Blythe, boys, I'd like you to meet Montana McFadden,' Tate introduced them. 'Montana is my foreman.'

'It's a pleasure to meet you, ma'am.' Montana tipped his hat towards Blythe, then with a twinkle in his eye added, 'I know what you're thinking. You're thinking that I should be six inches taller for my weight, but if you will consider the shape of the state of Montana for a moment you'll see that I'm close to perfect.'

For the first time in hours, she smiled a genuine smile and extended her hand in greeting. 'I'm pleased to meet you, Mr McFadden.'

'Montana,' he corrected.

'I'm Roger.'

'I'm Brian.' The twins stepped up next to introduce themselves to the second real cowboy they had ever met.

'Glad to meet you two. Even a blind man could see you were Calihans.' Montana beamed.

Blythe's smile faded and she turned to retrieve the luggage.

'It's been a long day. Let's get these folks to the ranch,' Tate instructed, relieving Blythe of the suitcase she had started to pick up and indicating that he wanted her to take care of the twins.

Tate drove, with Montana riding in the front seat and

Blythe and the twins in the rear. The sparsely populated country across which they travelled was rugged and hilly. In her present frame of mind, coupled with the bitter winter cold which seemed to have frozen the land in a grey gloom, Blythe saw the terrain as desolate and forbidding.

'Most of the people live in the urban areas,' Tate said as if he could read her thoughts. 'A man's not crowded out here.'

'Are we going to get to see any buffalo like at the zoo?' Roger asked, his hands resting on the back of the front seat as he sat forward to get a better view over the men's shoulders.

'I have a few that roam free on my range,' Tate answered. 'But the large herds were killed off long ago.'

'Were there lots of buffalo?' Brian leaned forward, too, like his brother.

'Why there were so many buffalo a single herd could take days to pass a given spot,' Montana informed them, turning to look at the boys as he spoke. 'Do you see those telephone poles?'

Both boys nodded in the affirmative.

'The buffalo loved those poles, only they weren't telephone poles in those days. They were telegraph poles then. Those telegraph men came along and put up their poles and almost before the wire was strung, the buffalo had discovered they made great scratching posts. Why, two or three buffalo could rub a pole out of the ground in only a few hours. I'll bet buffalo are the primary reason we don't have trees covering our prairie land. They probably rubbed them out of the ground before they had a chance to root.' The pronouncement was followed by a quick nod of the cowboy's head as he hurried on with his story before the boys could ask any questions.

'Anyway, those telegraph men got awfully tired of replacing the poles every couple of hours, so they thought they'd be real smart and they added spikes to the poles—sharp side out. Well, let me tell you, the buffalo loved those spiked poles. Old-timers tell me they'd see thirty or forty of those beasts at a time standing in line at every pole just waiting for a turn.'

'Mom, is he telling us the truth?' Brian whispered in an aside to Blythe.

'There were an awful lot of buffalo around here at one time,' she confirmed, though there was an amused quality in her voice.

'How'd you get the name Montana?' Roger's tone expressed envy.

'Well, now. My parents were the travelling kind of people. They never stayed in one place, let alone one state, very long, and to keep track of where they had been, they took to naming us kids according to what state we was born in.'

'What did they do if two of your were born in the same state?' Brian questioned, fascinated by this practical method of determining a child's name.'

'Now, it's real interesting that you should ask that.' Montana addressed the boys seriously. 'That situation did arise with my sisters. Twins, they were, just like the two of you. Luckily, at the time we were living in North Dakota so they named the first one out North and the second one Dakota.'

Blythe smiled in spite of herself while Brian looked towards Tate dubiously. Tate didn't seem to be paying much attention to the conversation. However, by chance, Blythe happened to look in the rear-view mirror and to her surprise found him watching her, a curiously questioning expression in his eyes. Turning away quickly, she pretended not to have noticed, and when she surreptitiously glanced back, it was to discover his shuttered look had returned.

They reached the ranch as the early winter dusk was settling over the valley, casting long grey shadows across their destination. The house was a single-storey, sprawling structure made of wood. Corrals and outbuildings were scattered about, all looking neatly kept and in good repair. Patches of ice lay here and there on the ground causing them to have to watch carefully as they made their way up on to the porch and to the front door.

Inside, the gloominess of the evening outside gave way to the rich warmth of polished wood and a brightly burning fire in the living-room grate. An Indian woman with steel-grey strands of hair running through the blackness of her thick braids came to greet them. Tate introduced her as his housekeeper, Ruth Fleetdeer, and the boys stared, enthralled by their first encounter with a real Indian. Blythe was embarrassed by their behaviour, but the woman didn't seem to mind. 'This house needs the laughter of children. Welcome,' Ruth said, then excused herself to finish cooking dinner.

Tate showed them the rooms they would be using. To Blythe's relief the boys' room had twin beds. She had been worried that they would keep each other awake if they had to sleep together. However, a frown crossed her brow as she looked more closely and it occurred to her that the beds had a very new look to them.

'Wow!' Roger exclaimed as he opened the closet. 'There're presents in here.'

'They're yours,' Tate replied and immediately the twins dragged the boxes out and began tearing off the paper.

Within minutes each boy had his new pair of boots and stetson on and was standing in front of the mirror feeling like a real cowboy. Sheepskin coats and warm gloves were found in the remaining boxes. 'Aren't they swell, Mom,' Brian beamed.

Blythe forced a smile before throwing Tate an accusatory glance.

'I wanted to be certain they were properly dressed when Montana gave them their riding lessons while I took you around to meet some old family friends.'

A defiant anger filled her eyes.

Back in the hall a few minutes later, Tate pointed out the door of her room which adjoined that of the twins.

'Are there any presents in Mom's closet?' Roger questioned.

'Roger!' she reprimanded.

'As a matter of fact there is a coat and gloves. I didn't know what size boot or hat, so I left those for later,' Tate replied.

Blythe wanted to tell him that there would be no 'later', but not wanting to confront him in front of the twins, she held her tongue.

'You knew what size to get us from that game we played where you measured our heads and drew the outline of our feet on a piece of paper, didn't you?' There was an excited gleam in Brian's eyes as he let the man know he had guessed his ploy.

'You're a clever boy.' Tate ran his hand through Brian's hair.

'Where do you sleep, Tate?' Roger demanded.

'Right in there.' The man indicated the room directly across the hall from the one Blythe was to occupy.

In the study the boys were fascinated by the racks of guns and horns mounted on the wall. 'Did you kill all of these animals?' Brian asked, wide-eyed.

'No. My father, your grandfather, was the hunter. I've never been able to bring myself to kill for sport.'

'Is this our grandfather?' Roger had climbed up on to a chair in order to examine more closely a picture hanging on the wall. Brian moved like lightning to his brother's side.

'Yes, it is.' Tate joined them, identifying the men in the picture as himself, his brother and his father. There was a stiffness in his manner which puzzled Blythe as she too moved towards the picture, uncontrollable curiosity guiding her feet.

Mike Calihan was slightly fairer in complexion than his brother and a couple of inches shorter. She also noticed that although there was some of the father in each of the brothers, their stance and manner were so different that it detracted from the family resemblance. The hairs on the back of her neck prickled and, glancing over her shoulder, she discovered Tate watching her, anger in his eyes. 'Excuse me,' she murmured, moving away from the group. 'I feel a little tired. I think I'll go to my room for a while and rest before dinner.'

Blythe did not, however, immediately go to her room as she had announced, but made her way towards the kitchen. She wanted to apologise to Ruth for her sons' behaviour. Not wanting to interrupt, she paused with the door open only a crack when she realised that Montana was in the kitchen with the Indian woman.

'I don't like what's happening to Tate,' the foreman was saying. 'He's getting tough as nails. He never laughs any more and he's got that woman scared half out of her mind, too. She puts up a good show, but her eyes remind me of that mountain lion we had to hunt down last spring because it was killing our cattle.'

'He's a good man, Montana. He's had to shoulder a lot of grief these past few years. I remember him as a boy. He was mischievous and headstrong, but there was a kindness in him, a gentleness. I saw that side of him again when he was with those twins. But you're right about the woman. She does have the look of a hunted animal around

the eyes.' There was a note of sympathy in the Indian
woman's tone. Backing away from the door, Blythe let it
close gently. Perhaps she was not as alone in the enemy
camp as she thought.

Suddenly she bumped into something solid.

'Eavesdropping?' Tate's voice was low and dangerous.
Turning her around, his hand covered her throat as he
forced her face upward. 'They both may feel sorry for you,
but they are loyal to me. Don't attempt to create dissen-
sion. As I have already warned you, I can be a very
dangerous enemy.'

Fighting to cover her fear, Blythe's mouth formed a
hard straight line. She hardly breathed as she met his
shuttered gaze.

The touch of the hand on her throat changed subtly
from a punishment to a caress. 'Damn!' he muttered,
abruptly releasing her and disappearing down the hall.

# CHAPTER EIGHT

DINNER was a quiet affair. The boys were almost too tired to eat and as soon as they were finished, Tate asked Ruth to take them to their room and put them to bed.

'I'll do that,' Blythe interrupted, rising from her chair only to be stopped as Tate placed a restraining hand on her arm.

'You haven't eaten,' he said, indicating the food sitting untouched on her plate.

Blythe remained silent until the boys were out of the room, then turned angrily towards the man. 'You're not my guardian and I'm no child. I don't need to be kept at the table until I've eaten.'

'You are behaving like a child. Do you think starving yourself is going to help the boys?'

Hastily she shoved a few forkfuls of food into her mouth. They felt like rocks as they hit her stomach. She knew she would be sick if she tried to force anything else down. 'There, are you satisfied?'

'No, but as you pointed out, you are no longer a child.' Rising from the table he left the room and Blythe fled to her bedroom.

Dressing in a heavy cotton nightgown she climbed in between the crisp white sheets and silently cried herself to sleep. Later in the night, long after all the others were in bed, she awoke with a terrible pain in her stomach. At first she tried to ignore it and go back to sleep, but was finally forced to leave her bed and seek a remedy. Pulling on her robe, she headed towards the kitchen hoping that a glass of milk would help. The curtains at the windows had been left open to allow the moonlight to illuminate the rooms thus eliminating the need to switch on any lights. Pouring herself the glass of milk, she retreated back to the living-room where she stood in front of the large window facing the front of the house and gazed out at the dark land-scape.

'Decided you needed a drink to help you sleep?' Tate's voice cut through the stillness. Whirling around she saw him in the doorway, his shirt unbuttoned above a hastily pulled on pair of denims. 'Fix one for me and I'll join you. I hate to see a lady drink alone.'

'I didn't know you were that fond of milk,' she said, wiping the mocking smile from his face.

'Milk?' His eyes fell on the glass in her hand for a more careful look.

'Sorry I'm not living down to your expectations.'

Running a hand through his hair, he passed her and poured himself a whisky at the bar. Then deciding not to drink it straight, he went into the kitchen and she heard him getting ice out of the refrigerator.

'You really have very little concern for other people,' she remarked coldly upon his return as he switched on the lamp near the couch. 'With all that noise you made in there, you probably woke Ruth up.'

'Woke Ruth up?' One eyebrow raised in an amused arch.

'I noticed her bedroom off the kitchen earlier this evening. I'm surprised she hasn't come out here to find out what all the racket was about.'

'I doubt if she even heard it since she's asleep nearly a mile from this place.'

'What are you talking about?' Blythe frowned, feeling suddenly very uncomfortable.

'I admit that Ruth does sleep in the room off the kitchen when the weather is bad or her husband is away, but as a general rule she prefers her own bedroom in her own home.'

'You mean to tell me that we're alone here?' She fought down the rising panic.

'Not totally. The twins are here.' His tone was pure sarcasm. 'You never fail to amaze me. You actually sound Victorian. For a woman with your past that's a real turn around.' Setting his glass down, Tate approached her.

When she started to back away, he caught her and pulled her up against him. Entwining his fingers in her hair he forced her head back, and her body trembled from his nearness. Holding herself stiff, Blythe fought the desire to run her hands over the naked expanse of his chest. As his lips began their descent, one part of her hated him, while the other waited with expectation for the contact to be complete.

Suddenly he released her, and retrieving his drink, downed its contents. Returning to the bar he refilled the glass, but this time made no trip into the kitchen for ice. Instead, he raised the glass in salute towards her. 'You've got nothing to worry about from me,' he assured her. 'I would never take you against your will. Besides, you belong to my brother.'

'I don't belong to anyone!' she threw back, then, in a slightly shaky, reasoning tone said. 'This idea of yours about my marrying Mike is ridiculous. It won't serve any purpose as far as the boys are concerned. They still won't have the Calihan name. He would have to go through the legal process of adopting them, and if he's as sick as you say, he will never live to see the paperwork completed.'

'You do have a point.' Tate frowned, setting his drink down untouched.

'I'm willing to be reasonable,' she continued. 'If you will let me take them back to St Louis and resume our lives, I won't object to your coming to visit as often as you like and then, when the boys are older, they can have their names legally changed if they so desire.'

'I'm afraid that won't do. As you pointed out to me some time back, Wyoming is a little too far to commute. Besides, I have a suspicion that the moment my back is turned you will pack up the boys and move, and I have no intention of playing hide-and-seek with you for the next few years.'

'I promise. I won't move.'

'I find it hard to trust you. However, I have been considering an alternative solution to our problem.'

'Then I don't have to go see Mike?' A spark of hope glowed in her eyes.

'He's dying and he wants to see you. He is the father of your children and my brother. I have no choice.' Tate's voice was hard with decision.

'Please, Tate.' Tears welled up her eyes. 'Don't I count?'

'Try to consider it duty. The man is dying. I am taking you to see him tomorrow.'

Holding the tears back, she carried her glass into the kitchen and placed it in the sink. Passing back through the living-room, she ignored Tate's presence completely. Later, as she lay in her bed, she heard him entering his room. Slow tears trickled down her cheeks. Saying a prayer that the next day would not bring her world collapsing at her feet, she tried to sleep, but it was not until the early morning hours that she was finally able to doze off.

Quiet whispering awakened her. Opening her eyes cautiously, she discovered her sons standing near the bed fully dressed and wearing their new boots and hats.

'Are you awake?' Roger addressed her in a hushed whisper, spotting her half-opened eyes.

'No.' She gave the expected response in this little game they had played many times before.

'Tate sent us in to tell you that Ruth will have breakfast ready in ten minutes. He says she hates people to be late.' Brian relayed the message with a serious expression.

Suddenly the sound of a large bell rang out. 'I'd say his timing was a little off,' she groaned.

'Come on, Mom. We don't want to make a bad impression and let her food get cold.' Roger tugged at her arm.

'You two go ahead. I have to get dressed.'

'Tate said you should come in your robe if you were still asleep when we came in,' Brian informed her.

'All right,' she agreed, feeling in no mood to try to dress quickly. Taking two minutes to run a brush through her hair, she then walked with the boys into the dining-room.

'We brought her like you said,' Roger announced as they entered.

'I'm sorry you didn't sleep well last night,' Tate's tone was almost apologetic. 'But I'm sure some of Ruth's coffee will make you feel much better.'

Blythe acknowledged his remark with a nod, but made no answering comment. Without really caring, she noted that he was dressed in well-cut trousers and a white shirt. This reminder of his plans for the day did nothing to help her mood. As she sipped her coffee, nibbled on a piece of toast and tried to clear the fog from her brain, he gave instructions to the twins. 'Montana will be here shortly to begin your riding lessons,' he said. 'I want you to be certain to tell him when you begin to feel uncomfortably cold, because I don't want to find two cases of frost-bite when your mother and I return. He's going to be here all day, so you can come in and warm up as often as you like then go back out again. Also, you are to mind Ruth.'

About the time the boys finished eating, Montana arrived. 'Brisk day out there,' he commented as he gratefully accepted the cup of hot coffee Ruth offered.

Both Brian and Roger tried to be polite and wait patiently for the man, but their fidgeting increased by the second. Subtly Brian tried to nudge him into action. 'Shouldn't we get started. You never know when the weather might change. It could even snow.'

'Why, a little snow never stopped a Wyomian.' Montana leaned back, tipping his chair precariously. 'I recall one winter when I was a boy, it snowed so deep that only the chimneys of the houses could be seen. People had to tie different coloured ribbons on them so you'd know whose house you had found. We even had to put snow-shoes on the horses and cattle.'

'How'd you get out of the houses,' challenged Roger.

'Had to cut trapdoors in the roof,' Montana replied.

'Mom, what do you think?' Brian asked, eyeing the cowboy dubiously.

'I think, maybe, you should be taking skiing lessons instead of horseback riding lessons,' she suggested.

'Montana on skis would be a sight to see,' Ruth commented with a chuckle, and was rewarded by a mock grimace from the cowboy.

Noting Tate's reticence during the exchange, Blythe glanced towards him, and for the first time noticed the deep lines etched into his face. He had not slept any better than she had. Curiously, this gave her a certain sense of satisfaction.

Montana and the boys left soon afterwards, and when Ruth returned to the kitchen, Tate broke his silence. 'Get dressed, Blythe,' he instructed. 'We're going to the hospital.'

'You won't reconsider,' she made one final plea, knowing even as she spoke that it was useless.

'You have twenty minutes. If you're not dressed by then, I'll dress you myself.'

Choosing a conservative navy blue suit, Blythe then applied a little more make-up than she would normally have used. If Tate questioned her, she planned to say that she was attempting to hide the traces of a sleepless night. Tate, however, made no comment.

During the ride to the hospital, she sat silently staring out the window. Not a whole lot registered on her frightened mind. Her main concentration went to keeping her breathing regular and her outward demeanour calm.

'Your brother has been asking for you all morning,' the desk nurse informed Tate as he passed. He merely nodded to acknowledge her information, never slowing his pace. Blythe ignored the curious looks she received as she walked beside him.

At the door of the hospital room she almost bolted and ran, but knowing that her only salvation lay in making it through this encounter, she entered slightly ahead of Tate.

'Your brother is very agitated this morning,' the private nurse announced on their entrance. Then, turning towards her patient, said in a voice not unlike a mother speaking to a petulant child, 'Your brother is finally here, and he has brought you a new visitor. I hope you will be nice.'

Although too weak to rise, Mike made the attempt anyway.

'Now, you just lie still,' the nurse directed. Then shifting her attention back towards Blythe, said, 'You will have to move closer for him to see you.'

Blythe hesitated while Tate held the door open for the nurse. 'We should like to be alone with my brother,' he said. It was a command and, although the woman obviously wanted to remain, she obeyed, moving out into the corridor. As he closed the door securely, Blythe approached the bed. The room smelled of medicines and death, and beneath the make-up she paled.

'Blythe.' The man lying there breathed her name, his eyes glittering with excitement. 'So he really did find you. I thought he was lying, especially when he told me you had kept the kids. But then Tate never lies.'

'Perhaps you overestimate your brother.' Her voice sounded strangely calm to her.

'Oh, don't get me wrong, honey. That wasn't a commendation—it was a condemnation.' Laughter followed this pronouncement and Blythe shuddered. 'Has he told you about his plans for us?'

'Plans?'

'Wedding plans,' Mike elaborated.

'He mentioned them,' she admitted, while vowing to herself that she would never give in to this demand.

'Well, I don't see much sense in it,' Mike chuckled. 'I asked and they won't let you share my bed.'

Blythe's hands tightened into tight fists and she took a step backwards.

'Mike, shut up,' Tate commanded harshly.

'He has no respect for the dying,' Mike addressed Blythe, ignoring his brother's warning. 'But then he has no respect for me at all. Did he tell you that I killed our father?'

'Killed your father?' Blythe thought she was going to be sick.

'Ask Tate to tell you. I'm sure he can tell it better than I can.' The dying man forced a yawn to show how much the subject bored him. 'Of course, you already know how violent I can be, don't you, Blythe?'

Blythe continued to stare at the man, but made no comment.

'What are you talking about, Mike?' Tate growled.

'I believe I overlooked mentioning that Blythe learned

to hate me before we parted. I seem to have that effect on people. I told you I had got her pregnant, but I forgot to tell you about beating her.' Suddenly the man began to whimper. 'It was the drugs.'

Blythe took another step backwards only to find herself against Tate's long length as his hands came up to cup her shoulders. 'I'm sorry, Blythe. I never should have put you through this. Why didn't you tell me?'

Still she remained silent.

'About the marriage,' Mike said snidely, drawing their attention back to the bed. 'I'm not going through with it. I have decided to make Blythe my final vengeance on you, Tate. You had me locked up and now I'm going to shackle you for life. To legitimise the boys, you will have to marry her, and the two of you can spend the rest of your lives in a living hell. I've taught her to hate the Calihan's with a vengeance, and your hate for me is so engrained that you won't be able to touch her without being sick because I had her first. Have a happy life.'

'I won't be anyone's vengeance,' Blythe stated sharply, and swinging out of Tate's protective grasp, left the room, followed by the man's insane laughter. She did not pause in her flight until she reached the car. Standing with her hands on the hood for support, she permitted the tears to flow freely. They were a mixture of disgust, hate and relief. She had survived the encounter with Mike Calihan and after what had occurred in that room, surely Tate would allow her and the twins to go back to St Louis and resume their lives.

'Blythe, forgive me.' Tate's voice was harsh as he turned her around and drew her into his arms. 'I should have guessed he was up to something when he told me about you. Honestly, I thought he was trying to repent for some of the damage he had caused in his short lifetime.'

For only a moment she weakened and allowed herself to

feel his strength, then reality brutally demanded that she reject his comfort. The man was still her enemy. His only interest in her was the boys and, although she had survived the ordeal with Mike Calihan, Tate was still a threat if she allowed him to come too close. Pushing out of his grasp, she wiped the remaining wetness from her face before it froze in the bitter cold. 'Will you take me away from this place?' she requested icily.

As the distance between them and the hospital increased, so too did Blythe's sense of relief. Glancing at her companion, she was shocked by the regret mirrored on his face. He was truly sorry for what he had put her through. Somewhere in him was a true gentleness she could no longer deny existed. But that tender core was so encrusted in layers of pain and hate that only the twins had been able to find it, and even they could not free it. If only she could have known him under different circumstances. As intense as her fear of the man was, a part of her cried out to help him. Blocking this dangerous emotion, she tried to concentrate on the passing scenery.

'He didn't tell me he had beaten you.' Tate broke his stoic silence. Glancing towards him, Blythe saw his eyes momentarily leave the road to fall on her wrist. 'I guess all of us Calihans have a tendency towards violence.'

Unable to permit herself to unfairly contribute to the man's suffering, she found herself justifying his actions on that night which now seemed so very long ago. 'You were defending yourself, Tate. That's not the same as slapping someone around for pleasure.'

Tate shook his head in the negative. 'I didn't need to be so rough. I was angry. I wanted someone to blame for what had happened to my brother, and I found you.'

'You blamed me for . . .' Blythe's voice shook.

'Don't look at me that way,' he interrupted harshly. 'I know I was being unfair. He was already on his downhill slide when he left home the day after his eighteenth birthday.'

Feeling the man's need to talk, she said in a softly coaxing voice, 'Did he simply decide that the time had come for him to leave, or had something happened?'

'He had invited several friends over for a party on his birthday. Dad walked in and found them smoking pot and threw them out and sent Mike to his room. That was the crux of the problem right there. He was always treating Mike like a child. Admittedly, Mike behaved like one, never accepting responsibility for his actions and always expecting other people to get him out of any scrape he got into. When he packed up the next day and left, we really didn't expect him to be gone long. He'd never taken care of himself before and we figured that as soon as his money ran out, he'd be back. When he didn't return after a couple of months we tried to find him, but having no idea where he had gone made that task impossible. My father had great hopes that Mike had finally grown up and was making it on his own.

'Then one day we received a call from a drug rehabilitation centre in Houston asking us to come and pick him up, so we did. My mother was dead by this time and it was only my father and me, but we did what we could. He had treatment, but he had got hold of some drug that had lasting side-effects that came and went. After a while, they were present more than absent. He was disorientated a lot of the time. I tried to convince Dad to put him in an institution, but he refused, saying that Mike was a Calihan and we Calihans take care of our own.

Then, one Thursday afternoon, Dad and I were out in the corral working with a new horse. It was a stallion and he was especially nervous. Mike came out of the house firing a pistol in the air and shouting something about space creatures. The horse bolted and trampled our father. It was an accident, but Mike knew what he had done. I had him committed after that. I didn't want anyone else hurt. That was five years ago.' Tate's delivery had been terse.

'And you've been carrying around this monumental guilt ever since.' Blythe studied the lean hard profile of the man at the wheel. 'I'll bet you say to yourself at least once a day that you should have insisted that your father institutionalise Mike, or that you should have been the one who was trampled. You probably spend hours figuring out all kinds of ways you could have saved your father in that corral.'

'You read minds?' Tate's manner was curt.

'No, but it doesn't take much to see that something has been eating away at you a long time. It's not healthy to dwell on the past, on what you could have done. You can't go back. You have to go ahead with your life. All of us have things we would change if we could.'

'My mistakes are not easily forgotten.'

'You've accepted the blame for something that was between your father and your brother, Tate. Don't allow it to destroy you.'

# CHAPTER NINE

'THANK you, Uncle Tate,' the twins chorused as they entered the house for lunch shortly after Blythe and Tate had returned from the hospital.

'You're welcome,' he smiled back, their youthful enthusiasm overcoming his tautness. 'How did the riding lessons go?'

'Terrific!' Roger declared.

'Tate had Montana find two ponies just the right size for us,' Brian explained to Blythe, his eyes bright with excitement. 'And they're really ours. We get to name them and everything. He even found saddles to fit us. Isn't that great!'

'Marvellous.' She forced a smile. Getting the Calihans out of her life wasn't going to be as easy as she had begun to hope on her way home from the hospital. Obviously, Tate was going to request some time with the boys. After a moment's consideration, she decided that that was only fair and he could have them a couple of weeks in the summer. The change would do them good.

'And there's a roan mare for you,' Roger interrupted her thoughts. 'Montana said Uncle Tate picked her out special to match your hair.'

'She was the gentlest of the lot,' Tate corrected briskly, as if he was embarrassed by the child's elaboration.

The noon-day meal was filled with detailed descriptions of the boys' first riding experiences and, immediately following the meal, Montana came for them to resume their lessons. Blythe, who had yawned through half the meal, excused herself to nap. It was almost suppertime when she awoke and went in search of Tate. She found him in his study, sitting in front of the fireplace, staring into the flames.

'I would appreciate it if you could arrange for the boys and me to leave tomorrow,' she requested. 'I'd like to get home and back to our normal routine as soon as possible.'

'We told them we would be here for a while. One day isn't "a while".'

'I hope you won't be offended if I say that for me it has seemed more like a lifetime.' Her tone was cutting.

'I've been considering our dilemma,' he said, ignoring her sarcasm.

'I didn't know we had a dilemma.' Blythe did not like the way this conversation was going.

'I brought you out here to legitimise the boys,' he reminded her. 'And although my brother didn't realise it, his solution was the one I had decided was the most reasonable. As you pointed out, marrying him would have accomplished very little at this late date.'

'I have already offered to have their names legally changed when they are a little older. But for you to marry me simply for the sake of giving them the Calihan name is absurd.' Her outward manner remained calm while inwardly she panicked.

'They wouldn't be gaining merely a name, but a father who would be around to help raise them, and you would have that security you were interested in when you agreed to marry George.'

'I thought George loved me and when I found out he didn't I called off the wedding.'

'You wouldn't have if I hadn't been around to needle you.'

'Maybe not,' she admitted. 'But I still think the marriage could have worked. George and I were friends. You and I can't even be in the same room without exchanging barbs.'

'You and George didn't even know each other, in spite of all the time you had spent together. If that marriage had taken place you both would have been unpleasantly surprised.'

'That's your opinion and it plus a dollar will get you a cup of coffee,' she retorted.

'If you are finished flinging insults, I think we should set a date for the wedding.' Tate's manner was indulgent.

'A wedding between you and me is out of the question.' Blythe folded her arms in front of her and frowned. She would not back down on this point.

'What's wrong, Blythe? Don't you think you can tolerate me in your bed?' He rose as he spoke, and with one long stride stood directly in front of her. 'I can be very gentle.'

Like velvet steel his hands circled her neck. Using his thumbs, he levered her head back and his lips descended on hers.

Knowing her lack of resistance to him, she pushed violently against the granite wall of his chest. In response, he deserted his hold on her neck and, winding his arms around her, pinned her to him in an imprisoning embrace.

Twisting her head, she freed her mouth from his tantalising persuasion. 'Let go of me!' Her foot shot up to meet his shin. Though he issued a mild moan, her action was of little consequence since the high leather boot he wore absorbed most of the kick.

'I like a woman with spirit,' he murmured against her neck, his breath igniting rivers of fire.

Straightening, he drew her upwards with him until her toes barely touched the ground. The hot tensed muscles of his thighs burned into her softer, more pliable flesh.

Blythe never willed her struggle to end, it simply ceased.

He felt her surrender and slackened his hold to allow her

arms to escape their confinement against his chest. Moving over his shoulders, her hands wound themselves into his hair.

Tate's mouth returned to tease her lips with light brushes until she strained against him, pulling his head towards her for a harder, more possessive contact.

His tongue teased sensually until her breathing was ragged and her desire so strong it was an intense hunger. She felt his hunger, too, and was suddenly frightened.

Sensing her withdrawal, he let her feet once again touch the floor and her body separate from his.

'I doubt if we will have any trouble overcoming your inhibitions to me.' A dark smile curled his lips as he gazed down on to her passion-flushed face. His hand rested along the line of her jaw while his thumb caressed her lips, still warm and moist from his mouth.

'I want something more than animal lust in my bed. I would feel used.' Her voice shook as she took a step away from him.

'You could consider it duty—something you do for the boys,' he suggested mockingly.

His words had the effect of a hard slap in the face. They told her that he saw her only as an object, that as a person he had no feelings for her other than contempt. 'No.' The word came from deep within her, filled with conviction.

'No?' He came towards her again, only this time she acted. Circling the couch, she used the piece of furniture as a barrier between them.

He stood watching her, the shuttered expression she had grown so used to, masking his face, preventing her from guessing his next move. The sound of the dinner bell suddenly broke the tense stillness of the room. 'We'll have to play games later,' he said in cool dry tones. 'Ruth hates for her food to get cold.'

Not trusting him, she remained where she was. With an

impatient shake of his head, he walked to the door and opened it. 'Come on.' His manner was that of an adult speaking to a petulant child.

Furious, she stalked past him and down the hall to the dining room. Eating absently, she kept her mind busy with schemes for getting away from him and his ranch as soon as possible. If he refused to co-operate she would ask Montana to take her and the boys to the airport.

'Mom, did you hear that?' Roger's excited voice drew her attention away from her plans for escape.

'What?' she questioned.

'Tate says we can go on an overnight camp-out with a campfire and everything as soon as the weather warms up. Won't that be great!'

'I suppose you could come back to visit during your summer vacation,' she said, emphasising the word 'visit'.

A dangerous gleam shone in Tate's eyes, but he said nothing to contradict her in front of the boys.

Using the twins' presence to prevent any further confrontations, she remained in the den with them while they watched television and played games. Tate had received a call immediately following dinner and did not join them, but went instead to his study.

By eight o'clock both boys were half asleep and gave their mother no argument when she suggested they go to bed. Too tired to risk facing Tate again, she also retired for the night.

The distant sound of a phone ringing woke her in the early morning hours. Worried that the boys, too, might have been awakened, Blythe climbed out of bed and, slipping into her robe and slippers, went into their room. Exhausted from the excitement of their day, both were still sound asleep.

Tate was in the hall when she came out of the room. 'Did the phone wake them?'

'No,' she yawned, noticing the tired lines around his eyes.

'That was the hospital. Mike's dead.' There was a tightness in his voice that told her this news, though not unexpected, was difficult for him.

'I'm sorry.' The words came out with feeling, but not for the dead man. For him she could feel nothing. It was Tate she was drawn towards in spite of the threat he posed to her. She knew what it was like to lose those closest to you. No matter how much sorrow they had given you during their lifetime, there was still grief.

'I could almost believe you mean that. You're very good with lies, aren't you, Blythe.' His tone was bitter.

Her facial muscles tensed. She knew he was lashing out at her because she was available, but still it hurt, perhaps because he was so near the truth. Turning away from him, she started back towards her room.

'I apologise,' his voice was harsh. 'Join me. I hate to drink alone.'

She knew he needed someone to be with him right at this moment and she was the only person available. Reversing her direction, she followed him hesitantly into his study. Pouring two whiskies, he handed one to her. 'Thank you, but I don't drink,' she said, setting the glass down. 'At least, not much more than a little wine.'

'Mike told me you could drink a man under the table. But then that doesn't fit your present image, does it?'

'You're being nasty, Tate.'

'I feel nasty. I've lost my father and my brother. Those two boys of yours are the closest kin I have now. Want to draw swords and fight for them?'

'No.' Her tone was cautious. He was in a dangerous mood. 'You can marry and have children of your own.'

'You can marry and have more of your own, too,' he countered. 'I'd rather stick with a known commodity.'

'The boys stay with me.'

'I made it clear that you were included.' He drained his drink and poured himself another.

Watching him, it dawned on her that he was still dressed in the same clothes he had worn to the hospital that morning, and when he recapped the decanter his aim wavered. 'Have you been in here drinking all evening?' she questioned, being careful not to sound judgemental.

'Not steadily. But I do confess to having had a couple, or maybe it was a few.'

'Do you think drinking yourself into a stupor is going to help?'

'I'm hoping it will blank out the movie reel running through my mind of Mike and me growing up. He used to follow me around like a shadow until he got into his teens and started hanging around with a bad crowd. I was too busy living my own life to do much about his choice of friends, except lecture him, and our father was doing enough of that. I thought he had more sense than to stay mixed up with that group. I keep thinking that if I'd given him more time, he wouldn't have ended up the way he did.'

'Life is full of "ifs", Tate. You're accepting a guilt that isn't yours. Mike ruined his own life, don't let him ruin yours.' Walking over to him, she removed the glass from his hand and replaced it on the tray. 'Come on.' Holding on to his arm, she led him down the hall and steered him into his room. Collapsing on to the bed, he lay staring up at the ceiling.

'Don't go. Stay with me,' he requested as she started towards the door.

'Tate.' Her voice was harsh with anger.

'I didn't mean it that way. I know I don't have any right to ask, but right now I need a friend.'

Frowning, she hesitantly retraced her steps. 'I'll sit in

here with you provided you remove your own boots and let me cover you up.'

Slowly swinging into a sitting position on the edge of the bed, he pulled the heavy leather footwear off. 'My mother used to use that tone with me when she was exasperated with my behaviour. Are you exasperated with me, Blythe?'

Unfolding the thick down comforter from the foot of the bed, she threw it over him. 'Maybe a little.'

'Maybe a lot,' he corrected.

'Maybe,' she agreed pulling a chair near the head of the bed and sitting down.

'Mike sure blew it. He had you and instead of loving you, he abused you. You could have turned his whole world around for him, and he threw it away.' There was a quality in Tate's voice that caused her to look towards him, but in the dimly moonlit room his face was a shadow. Reaching out he took her hand in his. 'For a while let me pretend that you don't hate the Calihans.'

A lump caught in Blythe's throat. She wanted to trust this man, but that was impossible. Painfully she recalled the morning after his return to St Louis. With the feel of his lips still vivid in her mind, she had heard him deny intentionally kissing her as if he was ashamed to have touched her. After which he had openly admitted that he would have gone to George and exposed her to stop the marriage. She should have been able to hate him for his arrogance alone, but she couldn't. She had tried. Sitting here with the warmth of his hand spreading over her, she knew that no matter how irrational it seemed, she loved this bitter man.

Swallowing the lump, she sat silently until his breathing was regular and she was certain he was asleep, and then she slipped her hand out of his. For a long moment she stood looking down on his sleep-relaxed features.

Then because she could not stop herself, she kissed his cheek softly before swiftly leaving the room.

'Sorry if I inconvenienced you last night.' Tate's tone was closed as he addressed her in the hall after breakfast the next morning.

'No one should be alone when they are hurting,' she replied, attempting to sound indifferent.

'Even a Calihan,' he added drily.

'I didn't say that.'

'You were thinking it, but never mind. The funeral is tomorrow and, for appearances' sake, you will attend with me.'

'Appearances' sake?'

'Ruth and Montana know you are the mother of Mike's children. They would expect you to attend the funeral. Unless, of course, you want to fill them in on the details of your relationship with my brother.'

'I will attend. Then the boys and I will be leaving.' It was a statement, not a question.

'You will not be leaving.' Tate's tone was hard.

'You can't keep us here like prisoners.'

'The West is one of the last bastions of male chauvinism,' he noted drily. 'And the boys are Calihans.'

'What if I swear they aren't?' Blythe knew she was grabbing at straws.

'A blood test will tell. Besides, you wouldn't want the twins to think that you were so unsure of their parentage that you changed your mind every week.'

'You are compromising me. Even if people think I'm your sister-in-law they will talk if we are living here alone. I'm tired of providing subject matter for the local gossips.'

'You will not be living here as my sister-in-law. You'll be my wife.'

'You don't even like me.' There was panic in her voice. 'Mike said it would make you sick to touch me.'

'I seem to have survived so far,' he pointed out. 'And if it starts to bother me, I'll simply close my eyes and pretend you are someone else.'

'How can you be so crude?' she screamed at him, hot tears burning at the back of her eyes. Slamming into her room, she stood holding herself while dry sobs racked her body. Brushing the single stream of tears from her cheeks, her mouth tightened into a hard line. He was not going to make her cry. Dressing against the chill weather, she left the house and walked towards the horse barn.

The boys were just mounting their ponies. 'We're on our way to find some buffalo,' Roger informed her, his eyes challenging her to deny them their adventure.

'You can come if you like,' Brian mediated, willing to compromise, but unwilling to relinquish his plans.

There was a lot of Calihan in them, she admitted to herself as she nodded for Montana to saddle her horse. The roan mare was gentle as Tate had said. Having learned to ride bareback in the northern farming country of Missouri, the saddle and bridle felt a little awkward at first. However, she adjusted easily and, within a short while, was riding comfortably.

The day was mild for this time of year. Still, by the time they returned to the house, Blythe wondered if she would ever feel warm again. The boys, however, didn't seem to mind at all.

'They'd make fine ranchers,' Montana told her as he led the horses away.

'Did you find your buffalo?' Tate asked the boys during lunch. Blythe noticed a preoccupied edge to his voice and realised that he was forcing himself to converse with them. Attributing the cause to his brother's death, she applied herself to her food. Not only was she hungry, but she fully intended to leave the table when the boys did and accompany them during the afternoon, even if it meant giving herself frostbite.

'Nope,' Brian's mouth formed a pout in answer to the inquiry. 'Montana says they are probably down on the south range enjoying the sunshine, but we're going to try again this afternoon.'

Roger nudged his brother. Brian responded with a sharp shake of his head.

'Is there something you want to ask me, Roger?' Tate questioned, watching the interplay.

The child looked up to face the man squarely. 'Do you really have palm trees on the southern range?'

'I see Montana is already corrupting these young minds,' a voice noted from the doorway as a man in a worn blue suit, carrying a doctor's bag, entered.

'What's he mean by that?' Roger questioned.

'He means you mustn't take Montana's stories too seriously,' Tate explained. Standing to shake hands with the new arrival, he indicated a chair at the table. 'I hope you have time to join us.'

'I've never been able to turn down one of Ruth's meals,' the man replied, accepting the invitation.

'Blythe, boys, this is Dr Marshall. He's an old family friend.' The intonation in Tate's voice on the last sentence told Blythe that the man knew who she was and who the children were.

'Is someone sick?' Brian asked, looking around the table.

'The doctor merely stopped by to meet you,' Tate said before the man could answer for himself. However, Blythe did not miss the mildly puzzled expression that flashed across the medical man's face.

'Did you know our father?' Brian asked.

'I delivered him,' Dr Marshall replied with a kind

smile. 'In fact, I delivered Tate, too, and I hope someday to be delivering a few more Calihans.' He finished by throwing Blythe a smile which left her feeling slightly shaken.

'We're Calihans,' Roger said, holding his head up proudly.

'Yes, I know. And fine-looking stock, too,' the doctor noted. 'Tell me about yourselves.'

This request was followed by a long-winded dissertation on their life in St Louis and their riding lessons. The discussion of their lessons reminded them of their search for buffalo and finishing their lunch, they asked to be excused. Tate nodded his approval. However, when Blythe began to rise to join them, she felt a restraining hand on her arm and, not wanting to create a scene, remained seated.

'Mom, aren't you coming?' Roger called from the door.

'In a minute,' she called back, throwing Tate a defiant glance, then added, 'You go ahead. I'll catch up.' In an apologetic tone she explained to the doctor that she had promised to help them locate the buffalo they were so determined to find.

'Well, my business won't take long,' he assured her. 'I'll just go down to the study and get set up.' Rising from the table he left the room.

As soon as the man was gone, Blythe turned to Tate, fire in her eyes. 'What is he talking about!'

'Have you already forgotten our little discussion this morning?' He answered her question with a question.

'Discussion? We had no discussion this morning. You made demands and I refused them.' She held herself rigid, her head high.

'Blood tests were mentioned, I believe,' he reminded her.

'Blood tests! You can't be serious. What will you tell the

boys? Besides, you were the one who was so sure they were Calihans in the first place.' Anger clouded her reason.

'We don't need to tell them anything right now. Dr Marshall will only be taking a sample of your blood today. So why don't you just be a good girl and march yourself into the study and get it over with.' His condescending attitude was the final straw and storming out of the dining room she made her way hurriedly to the study.

'Can we get this over with so I can leave,' she snapped at the medical man, startling him by her sudden entrance.

'Of course.' He indicated for her to sit down.

'I'm sorry I was rude a moment ago,' she apologised, unhappy that she had taken her anger at Tate out on this innocent bystander. 'I hate needles.'

'Most people do,' he replied kindly, accepting her excuse for her behaviour. The procedure took only a couple of minutes and was relatively painless. As she rose to leave he said, 'It's been a pleasure to meet you and the boys. Next time I come to lunch I hope I won't have to end it like this.'

Blythe nodded and left. Slamming out the front door, she jogged down to the barn, hoping the anger she felt would be burned off by the afternoon's shivering so that she wouldn't throw something in Tate's face at the supper table.

Again their search was futile and she informed the boys that it was her opinion that the buffalo were smarter than some humans she knew because they had probably found a warm place and stayed there instead of roaming all over the hills and valleys in the cold. Her sons didn't appreciate her attitude. However, she noticed that they did not object to sitting near the fire on their return to the ranch.

Immediately following dinner, she excused herself and, leaving Tate to spend the evening with the boys, went to her room. Sitting cross-legged on her bed she tried to sort out the situation in her mind. She had been in charge of her own life for a long time and it was ridiculous of her to simply wait for Tate's next move. The man was a dilemma. She felt uncontrollably drawn to him in spite of his harshness.

However, he had made it clear on several occasions that his interest was in the boys, and she was merely a member of the female species who happened to have some connection with them. She was the documented mother of the twins and no one was questioning her position in that role, especially after Mike Calihan's recognition of her. Surely Tate would realise he had no grounds for taking the boys away from her. She would reason with him. They could work out an arrangement for the twins to spend time with their uncle. Coming to a final decision, she slid off the bed and walked down to the study with the intention of calling the airlines and scheduling a flight back to St Louis the next afternoon. If Tate wouldn't drive them, she would ask Montana and call the Wyomian's bluff.

The room was empty. Looking up the number of the airlines, she was concentrating on dialling when a hand pressed the buttons in the cradle down and disconnected her.

'Exactly what do you think you are doing?' Tate demanded angrily.

'I'm making reservations for myself and the boys to return home tomorrow afternoon,' she informed him coolly.

'This is going to be your home and their home from now on.' His voice held no compromise.

'I have made it clear that they may come and visit you, but I will not be held a prisoner here.'

'If you were to leave right now you would find another "George" and be married within six months. That I cannot allow. You need someone to protect you from yourself, and the boys are Calihans and should bear the Calihan name. Since the best way to achieve both of these ends is for us to be married, that is what is going to take place.'

'Protect me from myself!' she glared at him incredulously.

'Left to your own devices, you almost married George and that marriage would have been disastrous for both you and the boys. He never would have been the father they needed and you might have ended up seeking an outside lover.'

'That's your opinion. I would have made that marriage work!'

'If you could make that marriage work then you can make our marriage work. With us it will be less of a struggle because the boys and I already get along well.'

Inwardly, she moaned. He had set a trap for her and she had fallen into it. 'You can't make me marry you.'

'If you refuse, I might feel compelled to seek other legal means to obtain the boys.'

'You wouldn't.' The fear mirrored in her eyes contradicted her words.

'Are you willing to risk it?'

'Your bitterness has made you cruel.' Her words came out in a choked whisper.

'Come now. We both know you don't find me repulsive as a man. I will be a good husband to you. I'll take care of you, treat you well, and as far as the boys are concerned no one else can fill the role of their father as well as I can.'

'I guarantee you will regret forcing me into this marriage.'

'If you would relax, I'm sure both of us could enjoy the arrangement very much.' His voice was low and coaxing. It was already too late to think of escape when she realised his arms were enclosing her. She stood stiffly, determined not to respond. She would show him what to expect if he continued to insist on this union. Drawing her gently against him as if she was a fragile china doll, he said, 'I've already told you, I will not force myself on you. I'll give you time to realise that this is the best solution for all of us.'

She felt his lips kissing her hair and was filled with a deep nagging pain. If only he cared about her as a person, things would be so different. But she knew his tenderness was only an act to cajole her into behaving. A single tear rolled down her cheek. He must have a great deal of contempt for her to think she could be so easily swayed.

'Roger, come quick,' Brian's voice broke the tense stillness of the study. 'Tate's kissing Mom.'

Blythe tried to pull away, but Tate's hold tightened.

'What's going on?' Roger questioned, coming to stand beside his brother who had approached the two adults.

'Your mother and I have decided to marry,' Tate informed them with a smile. 'I'll officially be your father then, if that's okay with you boys.'

'Okay? It's great!' Brian shouted enthusiastically.

'Does that mean we get to stay here? We don't have to go back to St Louis?' Roger's eyes were bright with excitement.

'Yes,' Tate answered, loosening his hold on Blythe now that he had enlisted the boys on his side.

Controlling her rage, she said through a stiff smile, 'Actually, Tate and I have to work out several details. We don't want to rush into this. I think it might be better if the two of you finished out your school year in St Louis. It would be less disruptive to your education.'

'Oh, Mom,' Roger's face formed a pout.

'Don't worry,' Brian assured his brother. 'I'm sure Tate can change her mind.'

'And I think it's time for the two of you to be in bed,'

Blythe directed, still retaining her plastic smile. In a slightly hysterical vein she recalled when she had announced her engagement to George. The males in this room had all been opposed to that union and it had not come about. Now they were united in favour of this one and she felt a sinking sensation in the pit of her stomach. However, she had fought them then and she would fight them now.

'Run along. I want some time alone with your mother,' Tate added his voice to her words.

After giving both adults hugs and kisses, they happily trotted off to their bedroom.

'That was unfair,' she hissed, as soon as the study door was closed.

'They had to know sooner or later. You do want them to attend the wedding.' Tate's manner was nonchalant, as if telling the boys had resolved the situation.

Trying another manoeuvre, she said in a more reasonable tone, 'Even if I do agree to this marriage, I still have to go back to St Louis for a while to make arrangements about the condominium and our things, and I don't feel right about leaving my job without giving notice.'

'You may return to take care of things after the wedding.'

'You are being bull-headed.'

'And you are sometimes untrustworthy.'

'Me, untrustworthy!' she retorted.

'You have a tendency to change your mind. You could decide not to return. Then I'd have to come after you, and I don't have time for such games.' Giving her a quick kiss on the cheek, he started towards the door. 'Goodnight, my love.'

Blythe stared at the retreating back until it disappeared. Hot tears burned behind her eyes. He wasn't going to have his way without a fight. Picking up the phone she again started to dial the airlines. A click sounded as one of the extensions was raised.

'Go to bed, Blythe,' Tate instructed.

Slamming down the receiver, she stalked off to her room. Tomorrow she would come up with a plan.

# CHAPTER TEN

IT was snowing heavily when Blythe woke the next morning. 'Looks like it's going to be a deep one,' Ruth remarked
as she placed the food on the table.

'If you want to leave early today, I'll fix dinner,' Blythe
offered.

'I'd take her up on that if you want to get home,'
Montana entered the dining-room, his face red and slightly damp from the cold wetness outside.

'I suppose this means we won't be able to go riding this
morning,' Roger frowned.

'Nope,' Montana confirmed. Then turning to Tate, he
said, 'Thought I'd run some extra feed out to the shelter
on the north range before the drifts get bad.'

'Fine,' Tate agreed, rising from the table and walking
towards the kitchen. A few minutes later he and Ruth
came out together.

'How would you boys like to help me this morning?' the
Indian woman asked, throwing Blythe a smile. 'I thought
we could bake a cake.'

Since riding was out, both boys readily agreed.

Tate watched as Ruth led them out into the kitchen.
When the door closed behind them he turned towards
Blythe. 'The funeral is in an hour. Be sure to dress
warmly.' Then, excusing himself, he went into his study.

Their destination, a white frame church nestled in a
valley with no other homes or structures nearby, seemed
lost in the middle of nowhere. By the time they arrived, the
snow was a thick blanket on the hills and roads. Inside the
building was only slightly less cold than outside.

'It's not normally heated during the week,' Tate apologised.

'If you keep us here, the boys are bound to find out about all of this,' Blythe whispered through chattering teeth as they sat side by side in the front pew.

'By the time they start seeing a lot of people, you and I will be married. Those who don't know the truth will think I'm the real father, and those who do know the truth will not gossip. We're a small community here and protect our own.'

Montana, having ridden over with them, finished paying his respects to the body in the coffin and joined them, cutting off any further remarks Blythe might have wanted to make. The doctor came in, followed by a large balding man in a black suit. With the appearance of these latest arrivals, the minister moved to the front of the church and began.

The wind howled outside as the snow continued to fall during the short service. On Tate's suggestion, Blythe waited inside the building while the four men in attendance carried the coffin out to the small cemetery in the rear. Returning shortly, they knocked the snow off their coats and hats and gathered together near the front pew.

'I'm pleased to meet you, Miss Walters.' The large balding man extended his hand in greeting. 'I'm Judge Anderson. It's a shame we have to mix both a sorrowful and joyous occasion on the same day, but here in Wyoming you learn to work around the weather.'

Blythe accepted the man's handshake while wondering what in the world he was talking about. She didn't have long to ponder.

'I've checked the papers the judge brought and everything is in order,' the minister said, joining the group. 'So Tate, if you and Miss Walters will step up here, we'll get on with this before the snow piles up so high you have to spend your wedding night here in the church with us.'

Panic made thinking impossible, as Tate took her arm and led her past the smiling faces to stand before the altar. Unable to believe this was real, she repeated the wedding vows as if in a trance. Any minute she half expected to wake up and discover it had all been a dream, a bad dream.

The minister asked her to remove her glove and when she did Tate slipped a ring on her finger. Then raising the hand to his mouth he kissed the gold band as if to seal his victory. A cold chill unrelated to the weather swept over Blythe.

'You may kiss the bride, but keep it short,' the minister finished the service with a laugh. 'I've had a lot of nervous bridegrooms in my day, but I don't think I've ever had a more tense bride. I've been worried through this whole service that she was going to faint.'

'She's not used to our Wyoming weather,' Tate offered with an amused smile as the wind shook the building causing the glass to rattle dangerously.

'Speaking of the weather,' Judge Anderson interjected as he approached the newly married couple. 'I think we had better get on with the signing of the certificate and be on our way.'

As soon as the document was signed each man claimed his kiss from the bride, and after wishing her and Tate a good life together, departed.

During the short time they had been in the church, the snow had completely obliterated their earlier tracks and Blythe realised that without a four-wheel drive vehicle, getting around in the winter would be next to impossible.

'I'll tell Ruth you'll drop her off so she won't have to call her husband to pick her up,' Tate addressed Montana as they pulled into the drive at the ranch. 'Then you'd better go on home yourself. We won't be doing much work today.'

'Will do,' the man agreed, then helping Blythe down from the truck, added with a broad smile, 'I hope you and Tate have a real happy life together, Mrs Calihan.'

She smiled nervously at the use of her married name.

'And when the weather settles,' the cowboy continued, 'the wife and I want to have all of you over for dinner. She's real anxious to meet you. Can't tell you how many times she's said that Tate needed a wife and family.'

'I'd like to meet her, too,' Blythe replied, hoping that Montana would attribute any stiffness in her tone to the weather.

In the house they were greeted by Ruth and the boys. 'Did you do it? Did you really get married?' Brian asked before they even had their coats off.

'Yes,' Tate answered. 'I'm sorry you boys couldn't attend, but the weather forced us to have the wedding a little ahead of schedule.'

'That's okay, Dad,' Roger said, his voice filled with pride as he used Tate's new title. 'We helped Ruth make you a special cake to celebrate.'

'They're very good helpers,' Ruth addressed Blythe. 'And I just want to say that you are getting a good man in Tate.' Then throwing Tate an amused glance, she added, 'Although he can be headstrong at times.'

'I've noticed,' Blythe managed to get out through her plastic smile.

'I left the lunch on the stove,' Ruth hurried on to explain as Montana helped her with her coat.

'Don't worry. I'll take care of everything,' Blythe assured her in a voice that held a conviction she did not feel.

'We'll see you in a few days, when the weather breaks,' Tate shouted as Montana helped Ruth into his truck. 'Don't worry about trying to make it back before then.'

'We understand. You want a little privacy,' Montana called back with a laugh, and with a final wave was gone.

Wrapping a protective arm around Blythe's shoulders, Tate moved her away from the open door and closed it securely. 'I don't want a bride with pneumonia.'

'I think I should check on lunch,' she said, walking out of his grasp and towards the kitchen.

'Wait until you see the cake,' Brian tagged along beside her with Roger and Tate following close behind.

Ruth had let the boys do the lettering. It was more than a little crooked, but the love that had gone into it made up for any defects.

'I wrote the "Congratulations",' Brian said proudly.

'And I wrote the "Mom and Dad".' Roger looked from one adult to the other, his face filled with delight.

'It's beautiful.' Blythe gave them each a hug, tears brimming in her eyes. 'Now why don't you two go and set the table for me while I see what Ruth has left for us.'

As the door swung shut after the boys, Tate drew her into the circle of his arms. 'We can make it work, Blythe.'

Refusing his comfort, she pushed away from him and walked over to the stove. With her back towards him she said, 'I thought you had to have blood tests to get a marriage licence.'

'We did.'

'What . . .' Suddenly the truth dawned on her as she recalled the doctor's visit the day before. 'You tricked me.'

'It was for your own good and the good of the boys.'

'You have no right to judge what is for my own good,' she threw back at him.

'Newly-weds shouldn't argue the first hour after their wedding,' he commented drily. 'It might set an unhappy trend for the rest of their married life.'

Biting her lip, she remained silent as she heard him leave the room.

The snow continued to fall all afternoon. Tate took the boys with him to the barn to check on the stock, after which the three of them played in the snow. Blythe watched from the window, her eyes filled with tears. Tate had backed her into a corner and she saw only pain for herself.

When they came in laughing and wet, demanding dinner, she made a determined effort to enter into their mood. She wasn't certain what she was going to do, but she did not want the boys to guess that anything was wrong. They were so excited. Nearly every time they addressed Tate they called him Dad and the warm glow in his eyes told her how much it meant to him.

They popped popcorn over the fire and played games until late into the evening. Catching a mocking glance from Tate, Blythe flushed. They both knew she was stalling for time. Finally the boys were practically asleep sitting up and she was forced to send them to bed. As she and Tate tucked them in a coldness developed in the pit of her stomach. In a moment she would be facing her husband alone and she was not sure what to expect.

'I'm tired. I think I'll go to bed,' she muttered as soon as they were in the hall.

'Sounds like an excellent idea to me,' he replied, catching her arm as she started to enter the room she had been using. 'You'll find your things in my room—actually, I should say our room, now. I had Ruth change them while we were gone.'

'Please, Tate. You promised you would give me time to get used to the idea of being married to you. I feel as if I'm in some kind of an incredible nightmare. You keep pushing one thing after another at me until I'm not sure what's happening.' Her voice shook as she delivered this plea.

'Nightmare?' The word came out in a low dangerous

tone as he roughly caught her chin and turned her face upwards to meet the cutting steel of his gaze.

Blythe's terror was mirrored in her eyes. 'You're hurting me.'

Releasing her as if she was suddenly burning his hand, he said coldly, 'You'll have your time. But you'll share my bed while you are adjusting.'

With a firm hand on her back, he guided her to their room. Finding one of her heavy cotton nightgowns, she went into the bathroom. When she came out a few minutes later it was to find Tate in bed reading. Slipping quietly under the covers, she curled up close to the edge, keeping as much distance between herself and the man as possible.

'You have nothing to fear from me,' he said scornfully, then slamming his book shut turned off the light and, lying with his back towards her, went to sleep.

Blythe awoke the next morning to the sensation of warm flesh against her cheek. Keeping her eyes closed, hardly breathing, she lay motionless, feeling the long length of Tate's body close to hers. In her semi-conscious state, with her mind still blurred with sleep, her physical desire for the man dominated her senses. He wore pyjama bottoms, but no top, and her hand resting on his chest luxuriated in the feel of the hard muscular expanse.

As he shifted into a more intimate position, his muscles rippled beneath her touch sending delicious waves of desire gently flowing through her.

'I know you're awake,' he murmured into her ear, nibbling on the lobe. 'I can tell by your breathing and your heartbeat.' As if to prove his point, his hand, which had been leisurely caressing her body, moved over her abdomen to rest on her ribcage above which her heart was beating wildly. 'I can feel it even through this blanket of a nightgown you're wearing. Can I assume that since you haven't tried to escape, that you have had enough time to adjust to our arrangement?' His mouth played over her face and neck as the words came out in a tone confident of the answer.

'No, you can't assume that and I haven't been awake long.' She pushed against him futilely.

'You're going to have to learn not to lie,' he warned with a mocking laugh as he pinned her down with his body and began unfastening the buttons on the front of her gown. There were only three which opened the neck wide enough for the gown to be slipped off over her head. 'Why don't you take this thing off,' he suggested huskily. 'Or let me remove it for you. That could be even more enjoyable.'

'Tate, you promised.' Tears overflowed from her eyes as she fought her hunger for him. If he did not let her up soon she would be lost. His mouth, exploring the exposed portions of her body, was making it difficult to deny him anything and as his hand sought her breast she began to tremble.

'Damn it, Blythe. I'm your husband.'

'Not by my choice,' she snapped back, surprising herself that she was able to speak coherently.

'Have it your way. I don't intend to rape you.' Rolling away from her, he lay on his back staring up at the ceiling. 'If you want to play the part of the innocent virgin being seduced by the big bad wolf suit yourself. We both know you aren't. Let me know when you're tired of playing games.'

Brushing the tears from her eyes, she threw the covers off and left the bed. Taking her clothes into the bathroom she changed quickly and went to check on the twins. They were watching television and ready for breakfast.

Tate joined them as she was putting the food on the table and a sense of electric tension suddenly pervaded the atmosphere.

Both he and Blythe pretended it was absent, but even the boys seemed slightly uncomfortable and confused. Following the meal he went outside to do the necessary snow removal and check the stock. The boys went with him, leaving Blythe to herself and her thoughts.

At first she tried to place all of the blame on Tate. He had pushed her into this corner by forcing her into a marriage so quickly she hadn't had a chance to talk to him, to tell him the whole truth. Then she admitted that she probably never would have confided in him if he hadn't already married her. There would have been no reason to and the risk would have been tremendous. If he had cared about her, things would be very different, but he had made it abundantly clear his only real interest was in the boys.

Thinking of the man caused her to glance out of the window. He had finished with the snow on the porch and was standing ramrod-straight gazing towards the mountains in the distance. There was a loneliness in his stance that caused her heart to go out to him.

There must be insanity in my family somewhere, she chided herself, fighting the emotion. How could she care for this arrogant man who commanded other people's lives with no regard for how they felt. Then, as if to prove her insanity, she found herself justifying his actions. She had confessed to him that she was planning to marry George for security and because the boys needed a father. He had simply, in his egotistical, chauvinistic way, decided to fill those needs himself.

At lunchtime, Tate hurried through his meal saying that he had a great deal more work to do before dusk set in. Blythe knew that wasn't the real reason. The real reason was that he couldn't stand being at the same table with her for any length of time. When the boys offered to help him again, he refused, explaining that he had to ride out to the south range, and with the snow on the ground it was too dangerous for a novice rider. They were disappointed, but found solace in building snowmen.

'We made four, one for every member of our family,' Roger pointed out proudly to his mother when she called them in for dinner.

Forcing a smile, Blythe peered out into the gathering dusk. Tate hadn't returned. Acting as if his absence was nothing to be concerned about, she fed the twins. Unable to eat anything herself, she explained that she would eat later with Tate. When they were finished, she built a fire in the den so they would be comfortable while they played.

Full darkness had fallen by this time. Only the moon reflecting its light off the snow offered any illumination. Standing alone in the living-room, peering out the window, Blythe's vision was blurred by tears. The thought that he had ridden out in this frigid weather simply to put distance between himself and her, preyed on her mind. She promised herself that tonight she would tell him everything and suffer the consequences. It was the only way. She was not stupid or naïve enough to believe that Tate would accept a non-consummated marriage. Also, she was not sure how long she could hold out against him. This morning had been difficult and it was only the first of many. If she allowed this situation to continue, the tension would build until irreparable damage was done to one or both of them, and then the twins would be hurt in the process. She couldn't allow that to happen.

Visions of him lying injured in a snow-drift filled her mind as she stood helplessly staring out into the night. She had tried to call Montana, but the lines were out and she had no idea where the man lived. Suddenly, a figure moving towards the house caught her attention. Blinking the wetness from her eyes she looked harder and was filled with relief when she recognised Tate. Running to the door she threw it open as he mounted the porch.

'I could almost swear you were honestly concerned,' he commented sarcastically as she helped him take his coat off. 'Or are you simply playing the role of the worried wife right now?'

Swallowing her hurt, she asked, 'Where were you?'

'The drifts were worse than I thought. It took a little longer than I planned to take care of the stock. I feel half frozen. Are you concerned enough to come to my bed and warm me?' There was a challenge in his eyes.

'We have to talk.' Her words were a plea.

'We never talk, we argue, and I'm in no mood for one of our baiting sessions right now. Since you won't warm me, do you think you could find it in your icy little heart to feed me?'

Following him into the kitchen, she began taking his dinner out of the oven.

'I'll eat in here,' he said, pulling a chair up to the kitchen table. 'And I can serve myself.'

She knew she was being told to get out and she did. Pausing in the living-room to wipe away the few tears that had uncontrollably escaped as she had left the kitchen, she proceeded into the den to inform the twins that Tate was back. From the relieved expressions on their faces she realised that they had been worried, too.

Although she was still determined to talk to Tate, she could not do it when there was a chance one of the boys might accidentally overhear. Her confession would have to wait until they were asleep. To help pass the time, she challenged them to a game of Parcheesi, then wished she hadn't as it dragged on interminably.

Tate never joined them. After she got the boys into bed and had read them to sleep, she went looking for him, only to find him in bed asleep, too. Her first impulse was to shake him awake, but her courage failed her. She hadn't yet come up with an easy way to explain her deception. Telling herself that she could face him better after a good night's rest, she changed into her nightgown and climbed into bed being careful not to disturb him. The restful sleep she wanted, however, evaded her. She tossed and turned, barely drifting off to sleep before she awoke again. Finally, her muscles sore from tension and a headache pounding behind her forehead, she crawled out of bed and made her way into the kitchen where she swallowed two aspirin.

Recognising the futility of trying to go back to bed, she wandered into Tate's study and curled up in one of the large upholstered chairs in front of the dead fireplace. Drawing her knees up under her chin, she tried to think.

'It's freezing in here.' Tate's angry voice cut through the darkness surrounding her. 'If you're going to spend the night in here, you need some heat.'

Before Blythe could offer a protest, he opened the grate and began building a fire. He was barefooted, wearing only his pyjama bottoms. 'You're going to catch pneumonia running around like that,' she said, feeling the need to make some remark, no matter how mundane.

'Then you'd be that widow you claimed to be,' he returned sarcastically as the logs began to blaze.

'I wouldn't want to see any harm come to you.'

Ignoring her response, he straightened and stood staring into the fire, his jaw set in a hard line. 'What is it about me that repulses you so much that you would rather spend the night shivering in a cold room than to share the warmth of my bed. Is it merely because I bear the Calihan name, or is it me personally?'

'I didn't come in here to escape from you. I came in here to think,' she sighed, too tired to fence any longer. 'I was going to talk to you earlier this evening, but you were asleep when I came back to our room.'

'I had no intention of giving you the pleasure of turning your back on me again.' His tone was bitter.

Running her hands through her hair, Blythe also stared into the fire. 'It doesn't give me any pleasure.'

'I was under the impression that revenge is pleasurable to those extracting it, and from what my brother disclosed, you certainly deserve your pound of flesh.'

'You're wrong, Tate. I don't want my pound of flesh, as you put it. I have no vengeance to seek against you.'

'I don't buy that.' His voice was taut. 'From the beginning your kisses, though unwillingly given, sweetened into desire. I saw it in your eyes. I felt it in your touch. I was so sure you were only holding me off because of pride and distrust. I married you to remove those barriers, but now you're even further away from me than before. You pull away from my touch as if I carried the plague.'

'It's fear,' she confessed shakily. 'Pure, unadulterated fear.'

'I'm not my brother,' his voice was harsh with emotion as he looked down on her. 'I would never harm you.'

'It's not that. I never knew your brother.' The words came out as if they were burning her mouth.

'He recognised you.'

Tightening her arms more securely around her legs, she tried to control her trembling. 'He thought he was seeing my sister. My twin sister.'

'You can't be Brenda Walters. The coroner made a specific identification.' There was anger in his voice as if he was fed up with her games.

'I am Blythe Walters, but it was my sister that your brother knew. She used my name. She always liked it better than her own and sometimes I think she thought of it as a joke. She is the main reason I try so hard not to categorise the boys. Our aunt was a great one for doing just that. She decided early that Brenda was the bad twin and I was the good one and treated us accordingly. I have always felt that a great deal of what Brenda did was related to living down to my aunt's expectations.' Blythe studied her hands as she spoke, unable to meet Tate's gaze.

'How did you end up with the boys?' he questioned tersely.

'Like your brother, Brenda ran away. Then one day she came back. Pregnant. My aunt was furious, but she was also very religious and likened Brenda's return to that of the prodigal son. Brenda refused to talk about the father. My aunt was at her all of the time, and the more she screamed at Brenda to give us the name, the more tight-mouthed my sister became. Brenda treated the pregnancy like a prolonged case of the mumps; as though once the babies were born that would be the end of the episode.

'She insisted on giving birth at a clinic where nobody knew us. After we brought the twins home she refused to have anything to do with them. Our aunt treated the whole situation as if it was a cross she had to bear. She and Brenda argued continually over what to do with the infants. I think Brenda would have gladly given them up for adoption, but their presence was such an irritant to our aunt that my sister refused that solution. While the two of them battled, I took care of the babies. They were so small, so loving. I fed them and bathed them and, for the first time since our parents died, I felt that there were other human beings in this world who were really a part of me, and I loved them.

'Then the accident happened. I had graduated from high school and had the house and some insurance money, so I told Dr Harley that I was keeping the children. He told me the courts probably wouldn't agree, but then the birth certificate came and Brenda had filled my name in as the mother. The doctor was the only person who could swear I wasn't, and I convinced him I could take care of them. We decided it would be best for all concerned if I left town, so I found a job in a bank in St Louis and went there. You know the rest.'

'I still don't see what . . .' The words died on Tate's lips as the truth dawned on him.

'I've never had children or been intimate with a man,' Blythe put words to his thoughts. 'I was afraid you would be able to tell. You've always made it clear that the boys are your only real interest. I love them, Tate, and if you take them away from me I don't know if I can go on. I feel like their real mother.'

'You are their mother. I would never have actually attempted to take them away from you,' he admitted tightly.

'Then why did you keep saying that you were going to?' she demanded, her voice choked with relief mingled with anger.

'Because after you found out who I was, it seemed to be the only way to keep you. I couldn't undo the things I had said and I knew I had terrified you so badly you would probably marry the first man to come along just to be rid of me. I hope some day you will forgive me. I'm not proud of what I did.' His voice was bitter with regret.

She stared at the man. 'Keep me? You don't even like me.'

'Do you think I would lower myself to blackmail, and go through all sorts of contortions to arrange a quick marriage to keep you here, if I didn't find you immensely likeable?' Approaching her chair, he knelt in front of her and took her hands in his. 'I admit I didn't want to like you. When I hired Harvey Adams to find you, I expected him to find a tramp. When he came back and told me he'd found a sweet, charming woman who was a good mother,

I was certain you had seduced him. Even after I met you, I refused to buy that loving mother routine. I kept watching you, waiting for you to show your true colours. When I saw you in those silk pyjamas, I was certain I had discovered the real you, but you acted so frightened and then you changed clothes. I was confused. You weren't anything like the woman my brother had described.' He pressed his lips against her hands while Blythe sat rigid, barely able to breathe. She had seen him as a threat for so long it was difficult to trust him.

'And I was frustrated,' he continued, tracing the line of her jaw with his fingertips. 'I had convinced myself that you belonged to my brother and yet I couldn't keep my hands off you. I felt as if I was coveting my brother's wife. It wasn't until I had actually told you that I was planning for you to marry him that I realised I would never allow that to happen. I couldn't bear the thought of him having the Blythe Walters I knew, even if it was in name only, on his death-bed. It was then that I admitted to myself that I loved you. Only I didn't realise how much until last night. Having you near me and not being able to touch you was worse than death.'

'You love me?' she questioned disbelievingly.

'I know I haven't acted like it. I promise I won't hurt you any more. I'm sorry for the damage I've done and if I could undo all of it I would. I won't hold you to a marriage you detest.' His tone was stiff, the words coming out jaggedly. 'I'm too tired to think right now, but tomorrow we'll figure a way out of this mess I've created. You can sleep in your old room tonight.'

She watched him leave, willing herself to believe him. He had said he loved her and the words echoed over and over in her mind. Reaching a decision, she walked purposefully down the hall to their bedroom.

The moonlight streaming in the window dimly illuminated the interior of the room. Tate was lying on his back and when she entered he looked towards her. 'What is it, Blythe?' he asked tiredly.

'You said you loved me. Were you telling me the truth?' Her voice shook as she spoke.

'If wanting to be near you every moment of the day; wanting to share my life with you; wanting to make love to you so badly it is a physical pain—if those things are love, then yes, I do love you.'

'Then I would like to remain here and be a real wife to you.' Her hands trembled as she unfastened the buttons of her gown and let the piece of clothing fall to the floor at her feet.

The moonlight silvered her body. Breathing unsteadily, she slipped in under the covers, but he made no move to claim her.

'As much as I want you. I know now that I cannot settle for a sacrificial lamb.' His voice was rough with emotion. 'I want you to want me, not just a marriage for the boys' sake.'

'I do want you.' Reaching out to him, she touched his hard-featured face. 'I was willing to settle for George because I never believed a man could make me feel the way you do. I've tried to hate you. I have been terrified of you. But always, inside of me, there was a longing I could not deny.'

Her heart pounded erratically as he lifted her to him. 'I want to hear you say you love me,' he commanded.

'I love you,' she admitted, her mouth moving against the sweetness of his skin as she surrendered to him. 'I love you.'

Blythe awoke slowly the next morning, a soft smile on her lips. Opening her eyes, expecting to see Tate lying beside her, the smile faded. He was gone.

She tried telling herself that he was not the kind of man who could lie in bed all day. But a glance at the clock told her that it was only seven-thirty. A tear trickled down her cheek. She must have disappointed him or, even worse, he had simply told her he loved her to get her back into his bed. The thought that it had all been a ploy to keep the boys tormented her.

Recalling how he had held her cradled in his arms long after their passion was spent, she tried not to believe he had lied. Her heart told her he loved her, but it mattered too much to her for her to trust her own instincts. She needed Tate's reassurance and he wasn't there.

Brushing the offending tear from her face, she crawled out of the bed and, going into the bathroom, turned on the shower.

As the warm water cascaded over her, she rationalised that it didn't matter whether he honestly loved her or not. He was the father the twins needed and she loved him enough for two. Still, she felt a deep sadness.

Suddenly she wasn't alone. Tate had joined her. Taking the soap from her hand he finished lathering her body, his hands caressing her as he worked.

'I leave you for a couple of minutes to fix the twins their cereal and make you a breakfast tray to sustain you through what I have planned for our morning, and I come back to find you have again deserted the warmth of my bed.'

'I . . . I didn't know where you were.' She gazed into the smoky grey depths of his eyes and her doubts vanished.

As if he guessed what had gone on in her mind he drew her into his arms. 'I love you with all my heart, Blythe, and I intend to spend the rest of our lives proving that to you.'

Tears of joy filled her eyes as she met his lips for a

tenderly possessive kiss. Then, turning off the water, Tate dried her and sent her back to bed.

She was sipping coffee and nibbling on a slice of toast when he again joined her. Opening a drawer in the nightstand, he produced a jeweller's box. 'I bought this on an impulse during my last trip home.'

Raising the lid, Blythe gasped as sunlight danced on the large square-cut ruby of the ring inside.

'It reminded me of your fire. Apparently, my heart always knew how much I loved you.' Removing the ring from the box, he placed it on her finger. 'I knew it was perfect for you,' he smiled. 'It even fits.'

'It's lovely,' she breathed, 'and I'll cherish it always, but not nearly as much as I will cherish the man who gave it to me.'

His lips brushed her mouth. 'I hope you're finished with your breakfast because I have a hunger which food won't satisfy.'

With a gentle laugh she welcomed him into her arms.